His re
had a price

"How long will you consent to let us stay on your land," Cara demanded, lifting her chin at a brave angle, trying to ignore the sinking feeling in the pit of her stomach.

"For just as long as it takes, *Cara mia*." Through slit lids Tyler watched her eyes widen with shocked expression.

"Don't call me that. I'm not *your* Cara." A traitorous imp inside her wondered what it would be like to belong to him, wholly and completely...to lie in his arms.

"One day you will belong to—"

"Never." She quelled the imp. "I detest you."

"Yes, so you've said before. But if you want the show to go on," he mocked, "then I'll be seeing you, *Cara mia*."

Sue Peters grew up in the idyllic countryside of Warwickshire, England, and began writing romance novels quite by chance. "Have a go," her mother suggested when a national writing contest sponsored by Mills and Boon appeared in the local newspaper. Sue's entry placed second, and a career was born. After completing her first romance novel, she missed the characters so much she started another and another.... Now she's as addicted to writing as she is to gardening, which she often does as she's formulating new plots.

Books by Sue Peters

HARLEQUIN ROMANCE

1975—CLOUDED WATERS
2030—ONE SPECIAL ROSE
2104—PORTRAIT OF PARADISE
2156—LURE OF THE FALCON
2204—ENTRANCE TO THE HARBOUR
2351—SHADOW OF AN EAGLE
2368—CLAWS OF A WILDCAT
2410—MARRIAGE IN HASTE
2423—TUG OF WAR
2471—DANGEROUS RAPTURE
2501—MAN OF TEAK
2583—LIGHTNING STRIKES TWICE

Never Touch a Tiger

Sue Peters

Harlequin Books

TORONTO • NEW YORK • LONDON
AMSTERDAM • PARIS • SYDNEY • HAMBURG
STOCKHOLM • ATHENS • TOKYO • MILAN

Original hardcover edition published in 1986
by Mills & Boon Limited

ISBN 0-373-02812-1

Harlequin Romance first edition January 1987

Printed in U.S.A.

CHAPTER ONE

'YOU'RE trespassing. Broadwater Park is private land.'

He swung his tall, golden stallion directly across her path, forcing Cara to rein to an abrupt halt.

'For goodness' sake!' She reined her spotted mare back on its haunches to avoid a collision. 'Why don't you give a hand signal, or something, before you cut in front of somebody like that? You nearly caused us to crash,' she accused the other rider angrily. 'If I'd been riding at full gallop, I wouldn't have been able to pull up in time. I might have taken a bad toss.'

'If you hadn't been day-dreaming, you'd have seen me coming. And it's to be hoped you wouldn't ride at full gallop across ground where a herd of milking cows is grazing. Or hadn't you noticed those, either?' he asked sarcastically.

'I didn't need to notice the cattle,' Cara responded haughtily. 'I knew they'd be there, the same as they always are.'

She thought she must have been blind not to have noticed the rider of the golden stallion. Together, the two made an arresting picture. The man's lean, tanned features were stamped with a lawless arrogance that would have sat well on a knight of the road, and his colouring was striking, to say the least.

Barred shadows from the bare branches of a nearby oak tree made tiger stripes across his rich, tawny hair, and a pair of keen tawny eyes looked authoritatively down into her own as their owner waited confidently for her to turn her mare round, and head meekly back in the direction whence she had come.

Cara surveyed him warily from under her thick black lashes. He was startlingly handsome. There was something about his face that seemed teasingly familiar, but she dismissed it as pure coincidence. If for nothing else—and there was more than sufficient of the 'else' by itself, she admitted grudgingly—his colouring alone would have an impact that would make any meeting with him unforgettable.

Her dark eyes took in his long, lean thighs, encased in tan-coloured riding breeches, and his tall, upright frame, shown off to advantage by a polo-necked sweater of the same shade as the breeches, and a faultlessly cut hacking-jacket that set off his broad shoulders and tight waist, that showed no signs of bearing a surplus ounce.

He sat his mount with the ease of someone born to the saddle, and man and horse made a perfect sculpture in bronze. A slender red setter appeared out of the trees and trotted over to join them, complementing the colouring of the two. Man, horse and dog matched almost exactly.

It was sheer vanity, to have a horse and a dog to match his own colouring. Cara sniffed. She loathed vain men. Reluctantly she had to admire his choice of animals. Both were obvious thoroughbreds, and in that respect too they matched their master.

'You knew the cattle would be here?' He took up her words alertly. 'I haven't seen you in the Park before this morning.'

Which implied that he rode through Broadwater Park himself each morning. Unaccountably Cara felt her pulses quicken at the information, but her voice remained cool as she answered, 'I always ride in the Park, whenever I'm in Broadwater.'

His eyes narrowed, assessing her, and there was a distinct ring of steel in his voice as he returned bluntly, 'From now on you'll have to do your riding elsewhere. I've told you, this is private land. There isn't a public bridleway through the Park.'

'I know that.'

'Then I suggest you turn round and go back the way you came. I'll let you off lightly this time, if you promise not to trespass again.'

Cara felt her hackles rise at his tone. 'How very condescending of you,' she bit back acidly. 'But for your information, the owner himself has given me permission to ride in the Park. In fact, I'm on my way to see Lord Broadwater now.'

This man must be one of the Broadwater Hall staff. Probably the new agent, she surmised. The old agent, a genial, kindly man like his employer, had been due for retirement when she last saw him two years ago, and this newcomer, with his air of arrogant authority, must be the replacement. The change was not for the better, Cara decided critically.

Her mare had fidgeted slightly to one side, nervously conscious of the close proximity of the stallion, and the movement opened up a gap in front of her. The warm stonework of the Hall loomed up a mere couple of hundred yards away, and the temptation proved irresistible.

Cara habitually rode without a saddle, and her slender body, moulded to the mare's bare back, made the animal under her instantly aware of any signals from its rider, and years of intensive training did the rest.

Impulsively Cara gave the spotted flanks the lightest touch with her heels, and nimble as a cat from its years of working in the circus ring, the mare took off under the very nose of the stallion.

If she had given herself time to think, Cara would have known she stood no chance in any race between them. The superior height of the stallion made only one long stride necessary, to the shorter mare's two, and the lightning reaction of its rider brought the big golden horse thundering in her wake before Cara had managed to cover many yards.

Urgently she pulled the mare to one side, trying to escape, but the other rider foresaw her tactic, and with a piece of superb horsemanship he followed her move as closely as if the two animals were harnessed in tandem.

With no more leeway left in which to take avoiding action, Cara was helpless to stop him as he reached down a strong, tanned hand and took the mare's rein in a firm grasp, slowing its gallop to a decorous canter.

'Loose my rein.' Cara turned furiously on her pursuer.

Already she regretted her impulsive act, recognising too late that she had played right into the stranger's hands by galloping close to the cattle, and laying herself open to justifiable criticism, as well as to the indignity of being overtaken and captured with such humiliating ease.

'You need to be taught a lesson,' the stranger told her grimly.

'And who's going to teach me? You?' Cara flared. 'The moment I see Lord Broadwater, I'll report your behaviour to him.'

'You do that,' the stranger invited coolly.

Ignoring her protests he retained his hold on her rein, and led the mare to a halt beside him on the gravel sweep in front of the imposing entrance to the Hall. Quick as a flash Cara slid off the mare's back, but the second her feet touched the gravel the stranger was beside her, his fingers taking her arm in a grip that made it clear he had not finished with her yet.

'Put the mare in one of the loose boxes, Joseph.' He handed the reins of both animals to a man in shirt sleeves, who came hurrying towards them from a nearby stable block.

'Hello, Joseph.'

Cara turned to the groom with relief, recognising the same man who had taken charge of her horse the last time she came to the Hall. The sight of a familiar face restored her confidence somewhat, and she smiled brightly at the newcomer.

'Why, Miss Varelli. It's right good to see you. I heard tell you were back.' The groom returned her smile with enthusiasm.

'It's good to be back,' Cara responded, and shook the gnarled hand held out to greet her. 'We got in last night. I've taken the first opportunity this morning to bring Lord Broadwater his tickets, as usual.'

'You didn't see the English newspapers while you were abroad then, Miss?' the groom asked slowly.

'No. We've been performing a lot farther afield this year. Way off the beaten track,' Cara answered. 'For a lot of the time we were in out-of-the-way places. We couldn't get hold of the English newspapers. We had to catch up with what scraps of home news we could, as and when we were lucky enough to obtain an occasional copy, which wasn't very often,' she remembered ruefully. 'I'll rely on you to bring me up to date with all the local news after I've seen Lord Broadwater.'

'But, Miss . . .'

'Give the stallion a good rub down, Joseph,' the tawny-haired man interrupted the groom. 'Miss Varelli will collect her horse when she's ready to leave.'

Without giving the two time for any further exchange, he increased the pressure of his grip on her arm, and propelled Cara firmly beside him up the entrance steps towards the studded oak doors, which were flung wide as a concession to the unusually mild November weather.

'After you.'

Only when they were actually at the door did he release her arm, giving her a mock bow, and standing aside so that she could precede him. Cara glared, and walked stiffly in front of him into the familiar entrance hall, the while resisting an almost unbearable urge to rub her arm, which tingled from his touch as if it had come into contact with a live electric wire.

'We'll be in the library, Daniels.' Her companion spoke to a middle-aged, tweed-clad man, another stranger to Cara, who appeared out of a door on the farther side of the hall.

'I'll have coffee sent in at once. The maids have lit the fire,' the man replied, and continued on his journey across the hall, giving Cara an interested glance as he passed.

'I fancy I may be about to light another,' the tawny-haired man responded with a quick upwards twitch of his well cut lips, and Cara shot him a startled look as his hand reached for her arm again, to steer her towards a door opposite.

Hastily she jinked away from his touch, and felt the tawny glance rake over her, reading her reaction.

Guessing the reason for it? She felt her cheeks grow warm, and broke into speech to cover her confusion.

'I know my way to the library.' With quick steps she made for the door and reached out her hand for the knob.

'Allow me.'

He forestalled her, and reached the knob first. His fingers closed over it, brushing against her own in passing, and Cara drew her hand back as if she had been stung.

She knew a childish impulse to suck her fingers to soothe the sharpness of the contact, and refrained just in time as he opened one side of the double doors that led into Lord Broadwater's favourite room. He swung the door free, then propped himself negligently against the frame, effectively narrowing the passageway, and there was an unmistakable challenge in his look as he gestured to Cara to go past him into the room.

She hesitated, measuring the gap with her eyes. Without him there, she would have had more than enough room to pass through, but his lounging stance took up quite half of the space, deliberately, she felt angrily certain. Her teeth caught on her lower lip, and she felt betraying warmth rise again in her cheeks.

To get into the room she would have to brush past him through the narrow opening, which was all the passageway he had left to her, but if she insisted that he remove himself to allow her more room, he would think she was afraid of the contact. Her chin came up.

'Excuse *me*,' she bit sarcastically, and stepped forward.

She would have dearly liked to sweep past him, but the confined space he left for her allowed no room for such a haughty gesture, and although she shrank as far to one side of him as was possible, she could not prevent her arm from brushing his sleeve as she passed by.

She was so close to him that her nostrils registered the faint odour of fine tweed from his hacking-jacket, and the infinitely more disturbing drift of an expensive after-shave lotion.

Her pulse began a slow thudding in her throat, and

impatiently she held her breath, resisting the dual assault on her senses, and then she was through the door and stepping sharply away from him into the familiar library.

'Put the tray down here, Jill. We'll manage for ourselves.' The tawny-haired man continued to hold the door open for a young maid bearing a laden silver tray, who followed them into the room.

'Will that be all, Mr Moncrieffe? I mean ...'

'That will be all, thank you, Jill.'

His smile put the young maid at her ease, and he stood aside patiently while she placed the tray with painstaking care on an occasional table. Cara stared. His smile had an unnerving sweetness that took her by surprise, like a glimmer of sunshine breaking through a threatening storm-cloud.

'The maid called you Mr Moncrieffe.' She hurried into speech the moment the door closed, grasping the initiative.

'It happens to be my name.'

'Tyler Moncrieffe, the naturalist?'

No wonder his face had seemed familiar. It also explained the reason why his unusually coloured hair and eyes had not struck a chord in her memory. The rarely used portable television set in her living-van was in monochrome.

It explained something else, as well, Cara realised triumphantly. Tyler Moncrieffe must be a guest at Broadwater Hall, not its agent, as she had supposed, and as a guest he had even less right to attempt to turn her out of the Park. The discovery restored her confidence to normal.

'Help yourself to coffee,' he invited.

'I didn't come here to drink coffee with you.' Cara faced him straightly. 'I came to see Lord Broadwater.'

'You're looking at him.'

'I'm ... *what*?'

Cara stared up at him, stunned.

'I said, you're looking at him,' he reiterated in a clipped voice. His glance suddenly keened. 'Sit down,' he said.

'I'd . . . rather stand.'

Her knees felt oddly weak, but even if she drew herself up to her full height, now they were standing together she discovered that her head did not nearly reach to his shoulders, and it rankled that she had to tilt her face up to look into his when she spoke.

'Just the same . . .'

He reached out nonchalantly to grasp the back of a nearby wing chair, and with a deft twist that scorned its weight he thrust the hide seat against the back of her knees, causing them to buckle and deposit her willy-nilly on its buttoned cushion. With the same economy of movement he poured out a cup of coffee, added sugar with a liberal hand and omitted the milk, and thrust the results into her nerveless fingers.

'Drink this,' he ordered her curtly.

Almost unaware of what she was doing, Cara drank, forcing the coffee down her closed throat as if trying to force down the unbelievable bombshell of information he had just dropped on her.

'You said you were . . . you are . . .' She choked into unaccepting silence.

'*I* am now Lord Broadwater,' he confirmed shortly. 'I inherited the estate, and the title, from my great-uncle nearly twelve months ago.'

'I didn't know . . . we've been abroad . . . we haven't caught up with the news in England yet,' Cara stammered.

'It's obviously been a shock to you.'

Cara nodded dumbly. Almost as great a shock was the implication of what had happened. As the new owner of Broadwater Park, he had every right to throw her off his land. With an immense effort she collected together her manners, along with her scattered wits.

'Condolences seem a bit belated,' she managed with difficulty.

'I haven't seen my great-uncle since I was a small child. I've spent most of my life abroad.' His tone rejected her sympathy, and Cara's lips thinned.

'I seem to have had a wasted journey,' she retorted. The coffee had done its work, and she put down the cup and gripped the arms of the chair preparatory to pushing herself to her feet.

'I don't see why.' The tawny eyes bored into her own. 'The title remains.'

Cara did not attempt to misunderstand him. 'The King is dead, long live the King?' she murmured sarcastically.

He inclined his head. 'Something of the sort. You told Joseph you had brought some tickets for Lord Broadwater.'

And the tawny-haired man was now Lord Broadwater.

Cara frowned her dilemma. She had liked the old Lord Broadwater. She had enjoyed having him attend their performances. It was her personal pleasure to deliver complimentary tickets to him whenever they came to camp in the Park, over-wintering there every year or so with the ready permission of its benevolent owner.

Her eyes measured his successor. His look was far from benevolent, and quite the opposite of the avuncular gaze she was accustomed to receiving from the Hall's previous owner.

She moved uncomfortably under the piercing stare, and dropped her lashes defensively, veiling her feelings. She did not like this newcomer, and she did not want to hand over the tickets to him, and thus invite him privily to become a member of their opening-night audience.

'Well?' he queried.

Was there just the faintest hint of menace in the monosyllable? Cara jerked back to reality. However much she might dislike him personally, he now held the title, and since the circus was camped on his land for the winter it would behove her not to go out of her way to antagonise him. It was sheer blackmail, but . . .

With fingers that felt stiff she reached reluctantly into the pocket of her slacks and withdrew the tickets, and without speaking she held them out towards him.

'Complimentary tickets?'

He smiled, accepting her defeat, and helplessly Cara gritted her teeth as he slid the tickets out of their envelope to read what was printed on them. She was totally unprepared for his reaction to what he found there.

'Mitcham Brook's *circus*?' he thundered, and waved the tickets accusingly under her nose. 'How dare you hand to me—to *me*, of all people—tickets for a circus performance?' he snarled. 'If I'd known you belonged to a circus, you wouldn't have come a step further across the Park, let alone into my house.'

It was like sitting on the top of a volcano, and having it suddenly erupt underneath her. His anger hit Cara with the force of a physical blow, and it was some seconds before she managed to recover her voice.

'What's wrong with the circus, for goodness' sake?' she cried bewilderedly when he paused for breath.

'Tell me one thing that's right with it,' he shouted. 'I loathe circuses, and all they stand for. Wild animals, locked in cramped, unsavoury cages, and only let out to perform silly, degrading acts for the pleasure of a gawking audience. You can go back to your circus, and tell this Mitcham Brook, whoever he is——' He gave a disparaging glance at the tickets in his hand.

'Mitcham Brook is the owner of the circus, and my uncle,' Cara stated proudly.

'Then you can go back to your uncle and tell him to remove himself and his menagerie from the Park without delay. I'll give him until tomorrow morning to pack up and be gone,' its owner declared. 'I won't have a circus camping on my land.'

His nostrils flared as if the whiff of caged lion and sad-eyed chimpanzee stank in their aristocratic depths. As if she was part of the same bad smell, Cara thought furiously.

'You can't turn us out of the Park,' she cried hotly. 'Your great-uncle always let us over-winter here.'

'What madness possessed him to allow such a thing was his affair.'

'But the fact is, he did. And because we've always been sure of our pitch here, we've got a full winter season of bookings already lined up in the district. We give our opening performance this evening.'

'Not on my land, you don't.'

'But we do. We *must*,' Cara insisted. 'The tickets are already sold out. We're booked absolutely solid for weeks ahead, and even when we close the big top at the end of the month, we've still got private bookings in the local stores. You simply can't force us to cancel everything at a moment's notice like this.'

'Just watch me,' he growled back. His tone was as inflexible as the granite-hard lines of his face, and Cara's anger rose to match his own.

'Your ideas about the circus are as out-of-date as the dodo,' she cried furiously. 'When did you last actually see a circus performance?'

'I've seen enough flea-bitten circuses to last me for a lifetime, while I've been filming abroad.' His expression was eloquent of his loathing and disgust.

'When did you last see a *properly run* circus?' Cara countered hotly. 'They're as much into the business of conservation as any naturalist, with your wild-life films, and your articles in the newspapers.'

'Circuses, into conservation?' he sneered disbelievingly.

'Yes, circuses,' Cara swept on, her black eyes flashing in defence of her profession. 'It was circus families who set up and ran the first safari parks. It's their lifelong knowledge of wild animals that allows them to breed from endangered species, and return them to the wild for naturalists like you to take your photographs.'

'That's only the tip of the conservation iceberg. A mere bagatelle,' he interrupted scornfully.

'Every iceberg has to have a tip. There wouldn't be one at all, if it weren't for the specialist knowledge that only the circus people can give,' Cara flashed back. 'Go along to any circus in this country, and you'll find people whose whole life is dedicated to the wellbeing of animals. My uncle is no exception, even though he doesn't keep a menagerie himself. We don't use wild animals in our acts.'

'Do you expect me to believe that?' he sneered.

'I don't care whether you believe it or not. It's true,'

Cara asserted. 'We haven't used wild animals in our ring since as long back as I can remember.'

She refused to tell him how long ago that was. Her twenty-three years were none of his concern, any more than was the reason why Mitcham Brook refused to work wild animals in his big top.

Doubtless the new Lord Broadwater would be totally unsympathetic if she explained to him that the last man to do so had been her own father, whose cardinal rule, 'never touch a tiger,' had been a byword in his profession.

In one second's inattention, all those years ago, he had accidentally broken his own rule, and paid the tragic price, and as Cara's mother had died in childbirth, Mitcham Brook and his wife took in the orphaned toddler and raised her as their own, and had steadfastly refused to accept any similar acts in their sawdust ring from that day onwards.

The man glaring at her now had the colouring of a wild animal himself, Cara thought. Tawny eyes, and tawny hair, like a tiger. Tyler. Tiger. There was little difference between the two, she thought with a sudden shiver. She remembered again the barred stripes that had lain across his hair from the shadows of the trees in the Park, adding to the illusion.

Never touch a tiger.

Why did she suddenly feel she had broken the same rule herself? Even as the thought flashed across her mind, he returned to the attack.

'I can't accept that you don't use the Appaloosa in the ring.' His eyes glinted in response to Cara's unconcealed start of surprise. 'Spotted horses aren't exactly unknown in the circus ring,' he reminded her, 'and your mare happens to be a fine example of the breed.'

'Of course we use Pride. She's a domestic pet.' Cara smothered her astonishment at his knowledge. 'We use the mare the same as we use our terriers. Those and the Falabellas are the only animals in our show.'

She mentioned the last deliberately in order to test him. It was one thing for him to be able to identify the spotted mare, but it was doubtful if his knowledge would extend to the lesser-known Falabellas. Her look challenged him to question her, and own up to his ignorance.

'So you keep miniature ponies, as well?' he drawled.

His knowledge matched her own, and to Cara's chagrin he scored easily off her somewhat obvious trap.

'My uncle breeds the miniatures as a hobby,' she answered stiffly. 'At one time they were practically unknown in this country, and he thought it was a pity to let the breed die out. He keeps eight of them in all, a stallion and seven mares, and he lets the foals go to breeders in other countries to help improve the strain. Like I said, circus people are keen conservationists.' She pressed her point home.

'You use the miniatures in the show ring, nevertheless,' he frowned.

'Of course we use them in the ring.'

Cara laughed suddenly. A burble of genuine amusement, that lit her eyes and her face, and for a brief moment the man's eyes fired, but she was too busy furthering her argument to notice, and the flame died as quickly as it had risen.

'That proves my point.'

'No, it doesn't,' Cara countered swiftly. 'The miniatures are family pets, the same as Pride and the dogs. They wouldn't allow us to leave them out of our acts, even if we wanted to. We've taught them tricks ever since they were babies. It's all just play, to them. If we went into the ring without them, they'd think they were being punished for some reason, and that wouldn't be either kind or fair.'

She watched him anxiously, trying to gauge his reaction to her spirited defence, but his expression remained closed against her, revealing nothing of what he was thinking.

Cara's forehead puckered. The whole winter living of the circus was at stake. Somehow she had to convince the late Lord Broadwater's heir that the circus must remain camped on his land until it was time for them to move on at Easter next year.

Her mind boggled at the alternative. There was no other such suitable site close to Broadwater, the small market town that would provide them with their audiences. It would mean a frantic search for a new place to camp, and the alteration of all their bookings and hand bills.

And what of the opening performance this evening? In spite of her thick sweater Cara felt suddenly cold. Would Tyler Moncrieffe stop them, with only a few short hours to go, and some of their audience probably already on their way?

'If you don't believe what I say, come and see our circus for yourself,' she cried, unable to bear the silence any longer. 'You can be your own judge.'

She did not make the mistake of assuming that Tyler Moncrieffe would ever be anything else. He would be judge, jury, and so far as the circus was concerned, executioner as well, if she was not able to stop him.

'I intend to,' he retorted ominously, and broke off as a discreet tap sounded on the library door. 'Come in. Yes, Daniels, what is it?' he asked, as the tweed-clad man Cara had seen earlier appeared through the opening door.

'Adams, the vet, is here to see you, sir, about the inoculations for the cattle,' the man explained. 'If you remember, you made the appointment because you specially wanted to have a word with him yourself.'

'Confound it, so I did,' Tyler Moncrieffe exclaimed. 'Now he's here, I'll have to see him. But cancel any other appointments I may have for today, will you? Something urgent has just cropped up.'

'Is it anything I can deal with for you, sir?'

'No, this is something I intend to handle myself, immediately after I'm through with seeing the vet. I'm going to visit a circus, Daniels.'

'Did you say a—a *circus*, sir?'

The man's reaction to the news matched that of his employer. Shock and open-mouthed disbelief registered in quick succession on his face, and if there had not been so much at stake Cara would have found the performance amusing.

It even brought a twitch to the set mouth of his employer, she noticed, but the movement revealed little amusement. It reminded Cara shudderingly of the twitch at the end of a big cat's tail, just as the animal was about to spring.

The sight haunted her all the way back to the circus, and she made the best speed she could to attend to Pride before hastening to her uncle's living-van, which was parked behind the big, brightly striped tent that housed the ring.

'Gio's been looking for you.' A woman came out of the tent entrance as Cara hurried across the grass, and she paused reluctantly to allow the other to catch up with her. 'He's been prowling round for the last hour, muttering about you wasting time riding instead of practising with him,' she said, her sharp eyes probing Cara's face.

'What's it to Gio if I choose to exercise Pride?' Cara responded defensively.

'You'll find out when you see him,' the older woman said maliciously. 'He was furious when you didn't turn up to practise with him in the ring.'

'He'll have to practise by himself for a bit longer, unless you go and join him,' Cara retorted sharply, and shrugged as her barb sent the other woman flouncing off in the direction of her own living-van.

Linda was nine years her senior, and after a back injury resulting from a fall in the ring, she was no longer able to perform on the trapeze, and bitterly resented Cara partnering Gio in a brilliant act that had once been exclusively her own.

She wanted Gio for other reasons, too, Cara suspected. Now Linda was no longer a trapeze artist, and the star attraction of the show, she had set her sights on marriage, and pursued the younger trapeze man with a relentless determination that was as pathetic as it was unavailing, Cara thought with a sudden flash of compassion.

It did nothing for her own relationship with Linda that Gio ignored the older woman, and pursued herself equally relentlessly, and with as little success.

What a muddle, she thought. And now this bother with the new Lord Broadwater on top of it. She hurried up the steps of her uncle's living-van. Why could not life be simple, for a change? If Gio married Linda, everyone would be happy, including herself.

But she guessed that Gio played for higher stakes than marriage alone, and the frown returned to her forehead as she pushed open the van door, and blurted out her news to her startled relatives.

Her description of the new owner of Broadwater Hall was bald and uncomplimentary, and she finished her narrative with a despairing, 'What shall we do if we're thrown out of the Park, Uncle Mitch?'

'There's very little we can do, except to move on,' Mitcham Brook responded worriedly. 'Now this new man's inherited the Park, he has the right to deny us access. What time is he coming?'

'He'd be here already, if the vet hadn't arrived in the nick of time. He cancelled his other appointments for this afternoon to give himself the pleasure of personally evicting us,' Cara answered bitterly. 'We can expect him to arrive at any time now, bent on vengeance. His man said the vet had come to see him about some inoculations for the cattle.'

'The Broadwater herd is a pedigree one, so he's unlikely to hurry his talk with the vet,' Mitcham Brook said thoughtfully, and looked at his watch. 'There's less than two hours to go now before we're due to start the opening performance. Don't say anything about this to the others. Just carry on as usual, and with a bit of luck the vet will delay Lord Broadwater until we're already in the ring. He can hardly turn an audience of two thousand people out of the big top single-handed.'

'Mitch, do you know where Cara is? I know she's back, because Pride's here, but I can't find . . . oh, there you are.'

A young olive-skinned man, with tight black curly hair and moody dark eyes, and the bulging arm and shoulder muscles of an acrobat, ran up the van steps and poked his head through the door without bothering to knock.

'You ducked out of practice this afternoon,' he accused Cara without preamble.

'You could practise on your own.'

'I can't practise our double act without you.'

'You go and limber up with Gio, and leave the rest to me,' Mitcham Brook interrupted the sharp exchange, and Cara stood up reluctantly.

'I'll have to change first. I'll join you in the ring in about ten minutes, Gio,' she told her partner, and to her relief the trapeze man turned without further argument, and went out with her uncle towards the big top.

The argument was only postponed, she knew resignedly. The moment they were alone together it would begin all over again, like a waterfall, persistently wearing her down.

'Have you upset Gio again?' Beth Brook wanted to know, and Cara made a rueful face.

'I'm always upsetting Gio, these days. He keeps asking me to marry him. I keep telling him no, but he won't take it for an answer, and his temper gets worse every time I refuse him.'

'Why don't you want to marry him?'

'Because it isn't me he wants, it's the circus,' Cara replied bluntly. 'Gio imagines that if he marries me, it'll be an easy route to him taking over the circus when Uncle Mitch retires.'

'It'll be a few years before that happens,' Beth returned placidly, and added with an obvious attempt to cheer her up, 'In the meantime I've made you a new bouquet for your opening performance tonight.'

'Oh, bless you.' Cara took the beautifully arranged bunch of paper flowers in its neat cellophane wrapping, and patted the large bow approvingly. 'The other one was a wreck. Pride stepped on it at our last performance.' She bent and gave her aunt a quick kiss of appreciation. 'Keep your fingers crossed that Lord Broadwater won't get here in time to stop the show, and I'll be able to use the bouquet. And now I must fly. Gio will throw a fit if I keep him waiting again,' she finished with a brave attempt at flippancy for the benefit of her aunt.

It dropped from her like a cloak as she reached her van, and her frown returned as she started to change.

She did not want to marry Gio. And yet, why not? She would have to marry at some time if she was not to remain single and lonely for the rest of her life, and she had worked with her partner now for the past two years, and knew him as well as she knew anybody.

He was young. Just three years older than herself. And he was undeniably good-looking. His work as a trapeze artist kept him at the peak of physical fitness, giving him a physique of which any girl might be proud in her man.

He was also ambitious, and unscrupulous in his determination to gain control of her uncle's circus.

Cara shook her head impatiently. She did not want to marry Gio. But come to that, did she want to marry anyone from the circus world at all? It was a small, enclosed community, with little opportunity to get to know anyone outside their own profession, so the chances of her marrying beyond it were almost non-existent.

Like a moving picture, Cara saw the pattern of her life if she were to marry within the circus world. She would have to relinquish her work on the trapeze when she had children, and cope with all the difficulties and discomforts of raising a young family in a constantly moving mobile home.

And when she had raised the children she would have to face the anguish of all circus mothers, and relinquish them to the care of strangers at a boarding-school, to ensure that they received an adequate education, an impossibility in a community that never settled in any one place for long at a time.

The gap after the children left would be even greater because, with her lissom body thickened by childbearing, she would be unable to return to her work on the trapeze, and her role would be reduced to selling programmes and candy-floss, or any other of the multitudinous out-of-the-ring jobs that the circus demanded.

Wistfully, Cara looked down at her new bouquet.

The reality of circus life was as different from the spangles and glitter of the sawdust ring as the paper roses were from garden-grown blooms.

Only the audience saw the glamour of the circus. The reality behind it was a life of unremitting hard work and sacrifice, with the women inevitably paying the greater price.

Her lips twisted. Whatever Tyler Moncrieffe's opinion of circuses might be, the animals led a far easier life than the people, she thought wearily.

CHAPTER TWO

HER black leotard moulded the firm, swelling contours of Cara's breasts, caressing her slender waist, and ending in close-fitting briefs that left her shapely thighs and legs free for their work on the trapeze.

She scooped up her shoulder-length black bob with practised fingers, and twisted it into a knot on the top of her head, slipping an elasticated snood over the results to ensure that no stray strands could escape, and wisp into her eyes at a crucial moment while she worked.

The stark severity of the style emphasised the fragile bone structure of her face, and the haunting quality of her huge dark eyes, but she passed her mirror without a glance, and was soon crossing the thick sawdust carpet of the ring, which presented a hive of activity as the performers practised for the evening show.

'I've put up your high-wire apparatus for you, Cara. If you don't want to use it now, it'll do for tonight,' one of the clowns called across to her.

'Thanks, Ben,' she responded with a smile. 'I'm going to work on the trapeze with Gio first, and then if I've got time I'll limber up on the wire.'

As well as performing on the trapeze and the high wire, Cara also worked Pride and the miniature ponies, and if necessary became part of the dancing troupe, a versatility demanded of most members of the circus in order to keep it to a size that Mitcham Brook could manage single-handed.

If she gave in and married Gio, her uncle would have somebody to help him who already belonged to and understood their strange profession, and to whom he could eventually hand over the reins of his business with complete confidence.

Cara sighed. She owed Mitcham Brook and his wife a great deal. But did she owe them this?

'Come on, Cara, we can't afford to wait all day. We've only got an hour at the most before we have to prepare for tonight's show, and there's still the rest of the apparatus to get ready when we finish, and the sawdust to be raked even.'

The energetic fooling of Ben the clown, and Poppy, his wife who acted as his stooge, was scattering the neatly raked sawdust into a condition as chaotic as her own thoughts.

'I don't feel like hurrying. It's stuffy in the tent.'

The stout canvas walls of the big top seemed to close in on her, hemming her in, and for the first time ever Cara knew a sense of claustrophobia. She felt an almost irrestible urge to run, as fast and as far as she could, away from, or to, she knew not what.

'You've never complained about it before, and we've been playing in places that have been a lot hotter than this all the summer. What's the matter with you?' Gio demanded impatiently.

She could not tell him because Mitcham Brook had warned her not to say anything, and hurriedly thrusting aside the vision of a tawny head and censorious tawny eyes, she ran lightly up the ladder to join her partner on the high platform of the trapeze. He looked down at her searchingly, but she avoided his eyes.

'Carry on. I'm ready.' She evaded his question, and after a moment's hesitation, in which she could feel the dissatisfaction in his stare, he set the trapeze swinging with an expert flick of his wrist.

'Start counting with me.'

The bar flew away, and then swung back towards them, and with perfect timing Gio launched himself from off the platform, and caught the horizontal bar, going into the routine of their act with fluid ease. Summoning up her reserves of concentration, Cara obediently began to count.

'One . . . two . . .'

During the actual show there would be music playing, and the rhythmic beat was designed to do their counting for them, but at practise sessions there was no music, and so they counted out loud together to

synchronise their timing, because a split second's
difference could mean a missed hold, and a horrifying
fall.

One, two, buckle my shoe. The childhood jingle ran
through Cara's mind as she counted, a throwback to
the days when she was five years old, and learning to
swing on the trapeze for the first time.

One . . . two . . . If she married Gio, there would be
two to carry on the circus when her uncle eventually
retired.

Three, four, shut the door . . . the jingle persisted. She
would shut the door on her freedom if she married Gio,
although no doubt her uncle and aunt would be
delighted to see an increase in their family to three or
four.

'Three, four, now!' Gio called.

Cara launched herself off the platform, and her
slender body, with its frail hold on the second trapeze
bar, plummeted through the air like a shadow,
following Gio.

If she married him, that was what she would become.
A shadow. His Latin temperament acknowledged no
such thing as an equal partnership. To him, male
supremacy was the natural order of things, and as Gio's
wife she would lose her identity as well as her freedom.

Automatically Cara swung upwards, and hooked her
feet over the horizontal bar, loosing her handhold and
allowing herself to hang upside down, the while flexing
her body to keep the trapeze swinging in time to her
partner.

The sawdust ring looked tiny, viewed from upside
down at such a height. She could see the clown spoofing
around, and hear his shrill shouts of mock dismay as
some trick went deliberately wrong.

'Five, six,' Gio intoned.

Expertly Cara altered the rhythm of her trapeze,
and Gio did the same with his so that they both swung
outwards, and then came together, rushing towards one
another at frightening speed.

Five, six, pick up sticks . . .

Gio picked up her hands as she reached out, loosing

her foothold on her own bar, and letting it swing away, allowing herself to fall, and relying on her partner's strength and skill to hold her safely.

'What made you so late, coming back from your ride?' he demanded to know as he swung her below him.

'How do you know I was late coming back?'

'I saw you go out, and I watched for you to come back. I always do. You're never longer than an hour exercising Pride.'

'I was this time. And you've got no right to time me.'

If she married him, Gio would not only have the right, he would exercise it. Again a sense of claustrophobia assailed Cara.

'Who kept you?' Gio demanded jealously.

'Does it have to be a *who*?' Cara flared angrily. 'I might have been simply enjoying my ride, and forgot the time.'

'To make you that late coming back, in my book it has to be a who,' Gio snapped.

'Oh, all right, it *was* a who,' Cara admitted impatiently.

For the umpteenth time her eyes flew downwards to search the tent, but her anxious glance saw only the tops of familiar heads. There was no sign of a tawny crown among them, and she let out a breath of relief. Every minute that passed increased their chances of putting on the opening performance, without Tyler Moncrieffe being there to stop them.

If only the vet would keep his client talking, just long enough to allow the show to get well started, they would be safe for this evening, at least.

A sudden, agonising pressure on her wrists brought Cara abruptly back to the present. Gio's fingers gripped them with a brutal force that made it feel as if the slender bones must surely crack. Pain seared through her arms, and she cried out urgently,

'Don't hold me so tightly. You're breaking my wrists.'

'I'll break more than your wrists if you play fast and loose with me,' Gio threatened ominously.

Cara stared up at him, her eyes widening. His teeth were tightly clenched together, grinding one another with the force of his anger. His face was darkly flushed, and it was not only because he was swinging upside down on the trapeze, suspending her beneath him.

This was more than the normal rush of blood to his cheeks. This was something different. Darker. Frightening. A cold thrill went through Cara as she gazed up at him, and Gio hissed at her furiously, 'Don't play tricks with me, Cara. I won't stand for it. You're mine, do you understand? Mine!'

'I'm not playing tricks.' She gasped at the pain in her arms.

'Don't try, or I'll make you live to regret it.'

If she lived at all, after a fall from this height. The thought sent another shiver through her. If Gio loosed her now she would drop like a stone. The safety-net was underneath her, but if he waited until they were at the height of their pendulum swing, the slightest flick of his wrists, undetectable by anyone who might be watching them from below, would be enough to fling her out of reach of the safety-net, straight into the serried ranks of wooden benches far below them.

Cara felt sick. Gio had an unstable temper, and if she goaded him too far he might be capable of . . .

'Who kept you?' The remorseless pressure on her wrists increased.

'It was Lord Broadwater,' she gasped.

Immediately the presssure relaxed, and Gio's fingers reverted to their normal firm hold.

'Oh, that old buffer,' Gio said contemptuously. 'What did he want?'

What would he say, Cara wondered shakily, when he discovered that it was not the old man, but the new Lord Broadwater? Young, exceptionally handsome, with tawny eyes and tawny hair, and in spite of his open hostility towards the circus, the kind of magnetism that put Gio's attractions in the shade.

'I'll tell you when we've finished practice. Let's get our routine over first,' she hedged. 'Seven, eight.' Deliberately she resumed counting.

Seven, eight, don't be late. She had been late, and Gio was angry, and he would be angrier still when he knew who it really was who had kept her.

'That's enough for now.' The moment they reached the end of their routine, Cara swung back on to the platform, letting go of her bar, and without waiting for Gio to join her she hurried down the steps to the ring.

'What's your hurry? We've still got a bit of time left yet before we need to pack up.'

Disconcertingly, instead of following her down the steps, Gio let go of his bar and dropped straight down into the safety net, and he was waiting for her at the bottom of the steps when she reached the ring.

Cara tried to dodge round him, but he forestalled her, and reaching out a rough hand he grabbed her by the shoulder.

'Don't grab me as if I'm one of the dogs.' Her anger boiled over at his cave-man tactics, and white-faced she flung his hand aside, her confidence returning now she was safely at ground level again.

'We haven't finished our practice yet,' Gio grumbled.

'I want to practise my backwards somersault on the high wire.'

With that Gio could not argue. The backwards somersault was a difficult and dangerous trick to do on the high wire, and even for a performer of Cara's skill and experience, it needed constant practice to retain the pitch of perfection needed to be able to perform it with safety in front of an audience.

As well, the high wire was one place where she could escape to, and know Gio could not follow her. Cara headed towards the waiting apparatus as to a sanctuary.

'What if I won't act as your catcher?' Gio threatened.

'In that case, I'll go up without one,' Cara retorted, and reached for the hanging rope.

It was against circus rules to work on the high wire without a catcher, and Gio knew it. As he also knew that he would have to account to Mitcham Brook if she went up on to the wire, and slipped, and he was not waiting below to break her fall.

'Oh, very well. If you must.' He gave in sulkily, and stationed himself underneath the end of the wire, and Cara slipped round him and shinned up the hanging rope with the speed and agility of a monkey, fearful lest he would change his mind and attempt to resume their argument.

A quick glance downwards showed him glowering moodily up at her, probably hoping he would put her off her stroke, she realised uncaringly.

Once on the wire she felt safe, and she moved across it with the serene grace of a ballet dancer, concentrating on the routine of her act. She danced, and skipped, and juggled the balls that Gio threw up to her, with faultless timing and perfect balance.

That done, she lay on the wire, confidently relaxed, then swung upside down underneath it, a move that always brought a gasp from the audience, and to finish her routine she performed three perfect back somersaults in order to make her excuse to Gio a valid one.

'Clear the ring, now. Time to clear the ring.'

Mitcham Brook's familiar shout, accompanied by a shrill blast of his whistle, brought all activity in the ring to an instant halt. Gio joined the other men in moving the apparatus, and Cara and Linda grabbed rakes and started to smooth out the sawdust.

'Where's Poppy?' Cara asked, when the clown's wife failed to put in her usual appearance to help them.

'I saw her going back towards her van.'

'That's odd,' Cara frowned. 'It isn't like Poppy to shirk work. Isn't she feeling well?'

'I don't know,' Linda answered indifferently. 'I know she's edgy. I heard her snap at Ben twice this afternoon.'

'It seems to be catching,' Cara retorted drily, and making sure Linda was not within earshot behind her, she hurried over to Mitcham Brook.

'There's no sign of anyone coming from the Hall yet,' he answered her unspoken question *sotto voce*. 'Beth's keeping a lookout. She'll give me a signal as soon as she sees any sign of a vehicle coming our way through the

Park. We'll open well on time tonight. With a bit of luck, we might beat your man to it.'

'He's not my man,' Cara denied hotly, and felt startled by the question that tracked unheralded across her mind.

What would it feel like, if he were?

There was still no signal from Beth heralding any movement from the Park as Cara began hurriedly to harness Pride and the miniature ponies ready for the ring. Familiar circus sounds reached her as she worked, the excited chattering of children already queuing up with their parents, impatient to enter the big top, their eyes wide on the coloured fairy lights that outlined the tent with carnival brightness, and put the early November darkness to flight.

Above the rattle from the diesel generator that supplied the circus with power came Poppy's voice, noisily scolding the hapless Ben for parking their living-van close to the generator, in order to save himself the trouble of a muddy walk to attend to the machine if the weather happened to be wet.

Cara made a grimace of sympathy with Poppy. The generator was noisy, but the circus had to carry its own power supply along with it, and Ben was responsible for its maintenance, hence his desire to park next to the machine, although Cara thought privately that Poppy's constant complaining was a high price to pay for the sake of the small convenience.

'Whoa, steady!'

She fixed the last of the bright head-plumes and spangled harness on to the skittish ponies, and slipped them a titbit each to keep them occupied while she hurried back to her van to change into her own spangled costume and headdress, ready for the ring.

The tent was packed. She took her place with Pride at the head of the queue of performers waiting at the ring entrance, and the opened flap afforded her a brief glimpse of the audience as Mitcham Brook, impressive in his ringmaster's garb of top-hat and tails, strode past them, and through into the ring.

His muttered, 'He's just come in,' as he went by her,

set Cara's nerves jangling, and then his deep, strong voice rang out from the centre of the ring, announcing the first act.

'That's us. Come on, Pride.' Cara vaulted to the mare's bare back, kneeling until she was clear of the entrance tunnel, and then leaping to her feet and balancing, light as thistledown, on the cantering mare, while the miniature ponies, their plumes nodding gaily, fanned out on either side of her in well trained co-ordination.

She spotted Tyler Moncrieffe immediately as she entered the ring. He was just taking his seat. The vet must have answered her prayers and kept him talking until the very last minute, she realised thankfully.

She knew exactly where to look for him, because the complimentary tickets were always for the same two seats at the ringside, but even if they had been among the crowded, cheaper seats at the back it would still have been easy to pick him out. His hair drew her eyes like a beacon.

A warning beacon.

Desperately she willed herself not to look at him, but his tawny head acted like a magnet and drew her eyes back to him again and again as she circled the ring.

The troupe of dancing girls followed her in, and then the clowns, tumbling about the sawdust circle in an explosion of highly organised confusion, making a burst of movement and sound and colour that got the show off to an action-packed start, a pace that would not slacken for any of the performers until it was over.

Unless Tyler Moncrieffe stopped the performance now.

Cara's ears strained, waiting for his shout ordering them to stop as the miniature ponies fussed through their routine, as self-important as children in a school play, and preening themselves before the attention of the audience. Her eyes swivelled anxiously to the ringside seats as she rode, but the new owner of Broadwater Hall sat silent, watching the activities in front of him with intent eyes.

Watching her, Cara knew tensely. She could feel his

eyes fixed on her, impaling her like a butterfly on a collector's pin.

The spotted mare stopped in obedience to the musical climax, and Cara slid from its back to take her bow, and her eyes lifted and clashed with the tawny stare from the ringside, defying its owner to take any action now, in the face of the wildly clapping audience.

His arms remained folded across his chest, she noticed, scorning to applaud their act. Angrily Cara turned her back on him, and leapt up to the mare's back again, and with a quick signal brought the miniature ponies in line behind her to lead them out of the ring, leaving it clear for the clowns.

Behind her she could hear Ben's voice raised in noisy altercation with the ringmaster. Mitcham Brook shouted back, and the clown pretended to weep, and the children, who comprised the major part of the audience, cheered him on, siding with the underdog as was their wont.

A burst of clapping heralded the end of the act, and Cara hurried away to change into another costume. A family of tumblers came next, and then it was the turn of herself and Gio on the trapeze.

With her usual economy of time she slipped into another costume, screwed her hair into a topknot, and popped a sequined snood into place before running to join her partner as Mitcham Brook announced their act.

'Cara and Gio, the daring trapeze artists. Watch them perform their death-defying feats . . .'

She could feel Tyler Moncrieffe's eyes following her up the ladder to the trapeze platform, and as she swung into the familiar routine they seemed to bore into her back like red-hot needles.

Destroying her concentration.

Her mind froze, blotting out the music, and registering only the piercing gaze that lanced upwards from the ringside seats far below her.

'Wake up, Cara. What are you day-dreaming about? You nearly missed your cue.'

Gio's urgent warning unlocked her feet from off the

horizontal bar in the nick of time, and his hands gripped her wrists with angry strength as he swung her beneath him.

'What on earth were you thinking about, to lose count like that?' he wanted to know furiously.

'I missed the beat. Lord Broadwater's in the audience,' Cara blurted out. Her nerves screamed with tension, jerking the truth unwillingly from her stiff lips. Her mind spun with questions. Tyler Moncrieffe had sat through her performance with Pride and the miniature ponies, without making any attempt to stop them.

Why?

Did it mean that the animals' top-class condition, and the obvious enjoyment they derived from their work in the ring, had settled any doubts he might have had as to their treatment in the circus?

Or did it mean that, because the show had already started, he intended to allow them to complete the performance for the sake of the audience, and then the moment it was over he would force them to pack up, and be gone from his land by the morning?

'What if he is here?' Gio demanded impatiently. 'Lord Broadwater's been to our shows before, and you've never let his title bother you to this extent. For goodness' sake pull yourself together.'

'I'm sorry.'

'You'll be sorrier still if you miscount, and have a fall.' Bluntly he used the dread of every trapeze artist to shake her mind back to its usual keen concentration. 'In any case, you're probably mistaken. I didn't see him myself when we came into the ring.'

Only because he had been looking for the wrong Lord Broadwater.

'The moment the show's over tonight, I'm going to have a word with Mitch and find out what's going on,' Gio threatened. 'You haven't made sense since you came back from Broadwater Park this morning.'

She might make very unwelcome sense to Gio, Cara realised uneasily, when he learned that it was no longer the old Lord Broadwater who inhabited the Hall, but his new and formidable heir, who had the right to dispossess the circus of their over-wintering ground, and who, in spite of all her efforts to thrust him away, seemed to have taken up possession of her mind.

The music rose to a climax and stopped. Their routine was finished, and fighting for composure Cara regained the ring and stood beside Gio to take her bow before she hurried back to take her place in the line-up, and use the brief respite to regain control of herself while the other performers entertained the crowd.

The human cannonball sat the audience on the edge of their seats with apprehension, and the clown rocked them back again, helpless with laughter at his artless tricks, until the sword-swallower effectively silenced them, gravely warning his young audience not to attempt the tricks for themselves when they returned home.

It was her turn to perform on the high wire next.

Nervily Cara wished she could opt out of the performance. The muscles of her stomach tightened into a hard knot at the prospect of appearing on her own in front of Tyler Moncrieffe. Once on the tightrope, she would be isolated by the merciless spotlight, without even Gio to help shelter her from that piercing stare.

'Cara will now perform for you on the tightrope.'

Mitcham Brook announced her, and there was no help for it. She had to go. Summoning up all her courage, Cara ran into the ring, and took her bow with a smile that felt stiff on her face, and vanished as she reached for the dangling rope.

Her nerves tightened until she felt dizzy, and she gained the wire with a gasp of relief that turned to one of dismay as she felt Tyler Moncrieffe's eyes pinpoint her again, like twin searchlight beams.

High up on the wire, she was trapped by his unnerving stare, and there was nowhere for her to hide. The watching eyes mesmerised her, sapping her confidence, and as she stepped out on to the thin strand she wavered, off balance.

'For goodness' sake, look the other way,' she begged the unseen watcher in an urgent undertone.

'What's the matter, Cara?' Gio's whisper hissed upwards, startling her out of her trance.

'Nothing.' Hastily she righted herself, and worked into the first stage of her routine, moving stiffly with limbs that felt like lead.

'What did you want me to look the other way for?'

She had not realised she had spoken out loud. 'It doesn't matter now,' she answered hastily. 'Pass me my skipping rope.'

She caught it with fumbling hands, skipped with less surety than usual, then handed it back to Gio and took the balls instead, and juggled with them, all the time tensely conscious of the watchful, tawny eyes, so that it was more by luck than good judgment that she did not drop the balls from her nerveless fingers.

If only he would look the other way. Or better still, go away. She heard her uncle's next announcement with a feeling akin to despair.

'Cara, the world-famous tightrope performer, will now attempt that most difficult and dangerous feat, three backward somersaults.'

Cara swallowed, her mouth and throat gone suddenly dry. In contrast the palms of her hands felt wet and slippery with nervous perspiration, and she surreptitiously rubbed them against the sides of her skimpy costume in an attempt to dry them lest they slip on the wire.

'If you don't feel fit, Cara, come down at once,' Gio commanded her from below. He had noticed her movement, and guessed the reason for it, and Cara hurriedly stopped rubbing.

'If I didn't feel fit, I shouldn't be up here,' she lied, and as Gio opened his mouth to argue she added crossly, 'For goodness' sake stop nagging. You're putting me off my stroke.'

She expended her venom on Gio because she could not reach the real culprit for her malaise. The music beckoned, putting an end to the argument, and in obedience to its beat Cara bent over backwards, reaching for the wire with both hands.

She went through the motions without conscious thought, her mind numbed by the knowledge that *he* was sitting below, watching her every movement.

The crowd sat in tense silence as she bent her slender body in a bow, as supple as a reed in the wind. Her feet left the wire and rose slowly in a graceful arc above her head, and carefully she swung then down behind her hands, back on to the safety of the wire.

'One . . .' Gio intoned from below her, and Cara bent again.

'Two . . .' her partner counted.

One more backward somersault to go, and she would finish her act, and be freed from the shackles of that tawny stare. The heat of it set her body on fire, but her hands remained as cold as ice, and her palms were wet again, with no time now to dry them. Cara was trembling as she bent backwards for the third time to grasp the wire behind her.

'Three . . .' Gio counted.

Her body arched. Her feet rose above her head, and she felt the wire wobble, responding to the tremble in her hands. Her feet came down towards the wire. She felt her left foot brush its taut hardness, before it continued downwards into empty air. Her right foot missed it altogether. She was falling.

'Aaah . . .'

The audience let out a long-drawn, collective groan, and the sound concentrated Cara's attention as nothing else could have done. For one brief, merciful second, she forgot Tyler Moncrieffe, Gio, everything except the disaster which was about to overtake her, and she reacted instinctively to years of rigorous training.

With swift presence of mind she doubled herself into a tight ball, and managed a quick mid-air somersault, and straightened out in the nick of time to make a perfect landing on her two feet beside Gio.

'Bravo! Bravo!'

Tumultuous applause broke round her, surging in waves of delighted clapping, and with commendable aplomb Cara remained where she had landed and took her bow, curtsying to Gio to include him in the applause, and neatly turning a near disaster into a triumphant end to her act.

It brought the whole of the audience to its feet in response to what they obviously considered to be a deliberate, nail-biting finale to an already dangerous act.

All, that is, except one.

Cara tried not to look in Tyler Moncrieffe's direction, but she could not help herself. He sat unmoving in his seat, his arms still folded across his chest, in the same position as before.

The spotlights were on the ring, highlighting herself and Gio, dazzling her. Although she strained her eyes to see beyond them, she could not make out the expression on his face.

'You were lucky to get away with that, without injuring yourself,' Gio said unnecessarily as they left the ring together.

It was too much to expect that the circus personnel would not be aware of what had really happened, Cara thought resignedly, and Gio reacted with typical censure.

'What on earth came over you, to make you slip like that?' he demanded.

Instead of rejoining the line-up himself, and leaving Cara to go and collect Pride ready for the finale, as he usually did, he kept pace beside her, away from the lights of the tent.

'I know what will come over me, if you don't stop firing questions at me,' Cara exploded angrily.

She still trembled from her near escape, and fright and nervous tension combined to bring her to flashpoint, and she rounded on Gio furiously.

'Something must have shaken you pretty badly when you went to Broadwater Hall this morning,' her partner persisted, and added an ill-timed, 'I've got a right to know what it was.'

'You've got absolutely no right.'

'I've got every right, where it concerns you,' he claimed belligerently. 'When we're married . . .'

'We're not married, and we never will be.' Cara felt safe enough defying him now they were both at ground level. 'I've told you, over and over again.'

'I intend to marry you, Cara.'

'Why don't you marry Linda, instead? She wants you,' Cara pleaded desperately.

'I don't want Linda. I want you. And I mean to have you, no matter how long it takes,' he growled.

'You don't want me. You want the circus.'

'So far as I'm concerned, you both go together,' Gio retorted unabashed. 'When I take over, I'll make the show we've put on just now look like peanuts, compared to what I can do. I'll bring the animals back. The elephants, and the big cats,' he boasted.

'Never,' Cara exclaimed. 'Uncle Mitch would never agree to such a thing.'

'When I'm in charge, Mitch will have no say in the matter.'

'You're not in charge yet, so don't be so ready to make plans,' she flashed back hotly.

With quicksilver speed she vaulted on to Pride's back and kneed the spotted horse past Gio and back into the line-up among the other performers, where no private conversation was possible.

She felt sickened by Gio's blatant aspirations, and yet caution warned her that she still had to work with him, and it would be unwise, even dangerous, to fall out with him completely.

Uneasily she remembered his veiled threat while they were practising together on the trapeze. Should she confide her fears to her uncle? Put baldly into words they might sound far-fetched and hysterical, and Mitcham Brook had enough to worry about with the threat of eviction hanging over his head, and it would not be fair if she added to his troubles now.

It would be better to wait, and see what happened after the performance. She thrust Gio and his moods aside in the face of the more immediate threat to the circus as a whole.

The minutes dragged by endlessly as the show worked its way through the final acts. Ben changed into a Mexican costume, and Poppy fluttered strips of ribbon for him to cut with a bull-whip, and the repeated sharp cracks of the thong battered at Cara's taut nerves until she felt ready to scream

The terriers worked next, jumping their way obediently through brightly coloured hoops before lining up in front of the ringmaster, each one ducking its head as if giving him a little bow as it took its place, and only Mitcham Brook saw the chocolate button that he dropped for each dog in turn, to cause the charming effect.

The finale came at last, and Cara took Pride and the miniature ponies into the ring, and the other performers followed her, until once again the sawdust circle was full of colour and movement.

The audience clapped and cheered, and her new bouquet landed in the ring, thrown by one of the circus staff strategically placed among the audience, and Mitcham Brook stepped forward to retrieve it, a distinguished figure in his black and white amid the colourful glitter of spangles and lights.

'God save our gracious Queen . . .'

The lights went up, the strains of the National Anthem brought the audience to its feet, and as the last notes died away the tent began to empty.

Tyler Moncrieffe was the last to go. He remained in his seat for what seemed to Cara an age, and when at last he rose to his feet he turned, and gave her a long, level look that sent a shiver coursing along her spine as Pride carried her out of the ring.

'Did you hurt yourself when you fell?' Mitcham Brook's hand on her rein detained Cara as she guided Pride out of the tent, and sharp on her denial he pressed keenly, 'What made you lose your balance?'

'It was my own fault,' Cara confessed frankly. 'I'd let that hateful man from Broadwater Hall get under my skin.'

'Go and bed down the horses. I'll see Lord Broadwater,' Mitcham Brook told her. 'I'd better get back to my van now, because he's bound to come looking for me there. I'll let you know what's happened as soon as he's gone.'

With that Cara had to be content as she unharnessed and fed Pride and the ponies. The sweet, musty scent of preserved summer tickled her nose as she hung up haynets for them to nibble, and made sure they had fresh water.

As soon as the animals were settled for the night, she turned wearily towards her living-van, pulling off her exotic headdress as she walked, and shaking her hair free of its constriction, grateful for the feel of the cool night wind on her burning forehead.

She would clean off her make-up and change into a sweater and slacks, although the hour was late. It would occupy the endless minutes while her uncle learned of their fate from the new owner of Broadwater Park, and give the latter time to leave before she went to her uncle's van to hear his news.

It would also ensure that she was dressed for any eventuality if they had to pack up and go immediately.

She tossed the headdress and bouquet on to her bed as she entered her van. She did not bother to switch on the light, the tent lights would burn for some time yet, and provide her with sufficient illumination for her needs if she left the door ajar.

She subsided on to a chair and reached for a tissue, and wiped her lips clean of their brilliant ring make-up. She was about to perform the same service for her cheeks when a shadow fell darkly across the van interior, blotting out the lights from the open door.

'Not tonight, Gio,' she called out irritably, without turning round. On top of the strain of the performance, to have to cope with Gio's temper now would be the last straw. 'I feel too tired tonight for . . '

'Too tired for what?' Tyler Moncrieffe's voice enquired smoothly.

CHAPTER THREE

'You!' Cara spun round, her eyes widening with startled dismay. 'Get out of my van. At once,' she blurted, too shocked by Tyler Moncrieffe's unexpected appearance to care that her words might exacerbate the already perilous situation of the circus.

Wildly, she wished she had put on a dressing-gown. She was still in her brief ring costume, but if it had been one of the circus people who stood in the van doorway looking down at her, she would not have given it a second thought.

In the presence of this man, she felt exposed and acutely self-conscious. Instinctively her hands rose to cover her bare shoulders, while hectic colour rushed to her face underneath her ring make-up, and she repeated furiously,

'Get out of my van.'

'To make room for Gio?' he suggested silkily, and took a further step inside.

Cara's colour vanished, leaving her cheeks chalk white, and causing her ring make-up to stand out in garish exaggeration against her creamy skin.

'How dare you?' she choked. 'What are you doing here, anyway? You should be seeing Uncle Mitch, not me.'

'I came to find out if you hurt yourself when you fell from the high wire tonight.'

Out of an audience of two thousand people, she might have known he would be the one to guess what had really happened to her act. Did he also guess that he himself had been the cause? The possibility made her burn with humiliation.

'I didn't fall. I jumped,' she lied defensively.

'And did your—er—jump, hurt you?'

'Of course not,' she retorted, scornfully. 'I made a perfect landing beside Gio. You saw for yourself.'

'Lucky Gio, to be in the right place at the right time,' he murmured provocatively.

'He's stationed underneath the wire merely as a precaution, against the possibility that I might be unlucky enough to have a fall one day. It's a recognised hazard of the profession, and has to be guarded against,' she informed him shortly.

'And is Gio another of the hazards of your profession?'

'Gio's my *working* partner. Nothing else.' Cara's eyes snapped at the insulting insinuation.

'As you say.'

His cool tone reserved judgment, and ignoring her gasp of outrage he toed the van door shut behind him, and came to lean casually against the end of her bed in order to ease the threatened crick to his neck if he continued to cram his too tall figure under the low roof.

'*Do* sit down,' Cara invited him sarcastically.

'Thank you I will.'

Disconcertingly, he took her invitation literally, and perched himself on the counterpane, first of all pushing aside her headdress and the bouquet to give himself more room to settle comfortably.

He seemed to fill the van, and Cara shrank back instinctively into her chair, her heart beginning to thud with slow, painful strokes. His move brought him directly opposite to where she sat, and across the confined space of the van his long legs brushed against her own.

'*Paper* roses?'

His eyes travelled across her taut unease, and came to rest on the bouquet, and their look condemned the artificial flowers.

'It's no use having real flowers.' Impulsively Cara defended the paper look-alikes. 'The bouquet has to be used twice a day, and fresh flowers wouldn't last from one performance to the next.'

'So the flowers aren't a spontaneous gift from the audience, after all?' His eyes returned to her face, and his brows arched as if he had just turned over a stone and discovered something unsavoury underneath, Cara thought furiously. 'Throwing a bouquet into the ring is just a piece of showmanship, the same as the rest of the performance? A sham, in fact, the same as the flowers themselves?'

His eyes travelled slowly over her face, noting the heavy ring make-up, and condemning that, too, for the same artificiality. Their sharp criticism drove her hands up to cover her vividly rouged cheeks.

'My ring make-up has to be larger than life and twice as colourful, so as to make an impact when it's seen from a distance. Just as it has to be on the stage of a theatre,' she said defensively.

She had no need to defend her make-up to this man, and she hated herself for her weakness in doing so, but the words seemed to be drawn out of her against her will, and she could not stop them.

'Does the person underneath the make-up have to be larger than life and twice as colourful as well?' he asked interestedly.

'Underneath my ring make-up, I'm just the same as everyone else.'

'Are you? I wonder.' He gave her a long, considering look that made her pulses race with sudden apprehension. 'It would be interesting to find out,' he said with a satirical twist of his lips.

'Better men than you have tried and failed,' Cara flashed back recklessly.

'Better men than Gio?'

It was too late to regret her rashness. With rising panic Cara saw him lean forward. She had a swift vision of his tawny head outlined against the tent lights beyond the van window, before they were blotted out as his hands reached towards her.

'Perhaps Gio isn't the kind of man to respond to a challenge?' he purred.

If Gio was not the type, clearly Tyler Moncrieffe was.

He grasped her with hard hands, and lifted her towards him, and his touch galvanised Cara into explosive life.

'Let me go!'

Frantically she pummelled at him with her fists,

trying to fend him off, fighting like a wild thing in the steel trap of his hold. His low laugh goaded her to fury as he held her easily, with no more apparent effort than if she had been a child.

'Let me go.'

'I thought you said you'd got no wild animals in your circus,' he mocked her struggles.

'We haven't,' she panted. 'You've seen all the animals we've got, in the ring tonight. There's nothing wilder than dogs and ponies. Family pets.'

'Nothing wilder on *four feet*,' he taunted, and bent his head above her.

Desperately Cara twisted her head from side to side, trying to escape him, and unhurriedly he shifted his hands to hold her with a firmer grip. One arm closed round her waist, clamping her to him, so close that she could feel the taut, hard strength of his body pressed against her own.

The contact sent the blood leaping in her veins as he captured her head with his other hand, forcing her into stillness.

'No!'

She pressed her hands against his chest, trying to push him away, but she was as helpless as a kitten against his superior strength.

'Yes, Cara,' he mocked, and brought his lips down hard upon her mouth.

With a low moan she closed her eyes, her black-lashed lids her only remaining defence against him. Shrinkingly she felt his lips close over her own, firm, masterful, exploring her mouth with a deadly expertise that sent shudders of unwilling response through her trembling body.

With fine-tuned awareness he sensed her response, and his kiss changed and deepened, teasing the dimpled corner of her mouth, and trailing fire across her soft lips.

Desperately Cara tried to steel herself to remain stiff and unyielding in his arms, fighting the leaping flames that raged through her veins like a bush fire, melting her resistance, and turning her muscles to water.

'Cara . . .'

His voice was husky on her name. The strong, steady throb of his heartbeat like a drum in her ear, and the faint, remembered smell of his after-shave lotion acted like a drug on her swimming senses.

She felt herself weaken, her body going pliant in his arms, and with a low laugh of triumph he bent her expertly backwards, the better to bring up her face to meet his own, plundering her lips, that responded with a will of their own as they drank in the heady wine of his kisses.

She quivered under his touch as his lips began a voyage of discovery across her cheeks, her eyes, her hair, tipping her head still further backwards to tantalise the long, slender column of her throat. Of their own volition, her hands began to rise, to clasp themselves behind his head, seeking to draw his mouth back to her own.

'I think there might be a real person underneath the make-up after all, if somebody took the trouble to dig deeply enough to find out,' he taunted, and lifted her with swift ease, and set her back again on her own chair.

'I didn't invite you to try.' Cara's glare scorched him across the van, and she smoothed down her tumbled hair with hands that shook. 'Get out of my van,' she commanded him shrilly.

'And leave the field clear for Gio?' he mocked.

Cara's head snapped up, her eyes flashing. 'Gio doesn't come to my van at this time of night, ever,' she denied hotly.

'Which leaves him all the rest of the twenty-four hours in which to try.'

'You . . .' In an excess of rage, Cara raised her hand, and aimed a blow at his head.

'You little wildcat!'

He fielded her fist with frightening ease, and held on to it, resisting her struggles to pull herself free.

'Let me go!' she shouted.

'If you try that again, I might be tempted to retaliate in kind,' he warned her grimly.

He let her go, suddenly and without any warning. Her chair tipped backwards alarmingly, off-balanced by her struggles to free herself, and Cara righted it with an undignified lurch, furiously conscious of his mocking grin as he surveyed her struggle, making no attempt to help her.

'I loathe you,' she gasped fiercely.

His eyes narrowed to thin, golden slits, between lashes that, she saw, startled, were long and thick, and would be the envy of many a girl. 'Carry on loathing, my little wildcat,' he told her softly. 'It might be an interesting experiment to tame you.'

'Men have been known to lose their lives, trying to tame wildcats,' she spat back.

'Some men, like Gio for instance, might take that as a warning.'

'Heed it yourself, if you don't want to risk getting clawed.'

'To me it sounds more like an invitation.' He laughed suddenly, a low, musical taunt that set Cara's teeth on edge, and before she could prevent him he bent and kissed her again, lightly, on her lips. 'An invitation I accept, Cara,' he said softly.

There was a menacing undertone to his voice that brought her eyes up swiftly to his face.

'You've used up the only invitation you'll get,' she flung back. 'The complimentary tickets are for the one performance only.'

'But there'll be other performances, Cara. Personal ones, for my sole benefit.'

'You've no right to come to the circus without permission.'

'I don't wait for permission. I go where I please, when I please, especially on my own land.'

And the circus was camped on Tyler Moncrieffe's land.

With a sense of shock Cara recollected the reason he had come to the circus in the first place.

'How long are you going to condescend to let us stay on your land?' she demanded, tilting her chin at a brave angle, and trying to ignore the sinking feeling in the pit of her stomach.

'For just as long as it takes, Cara.' Through slit lids he watched her eyes widen with shocked comprehension, then he went on, 'What better reason could a naturalist have for allowing a circus to camp on his land, than to spend the winter taming a wildcat?'

'Don't call me Cara. I didn't give you permission to use my first name.'

'Why not, Cara?' He rolled her name round his tongue slowly, deliberately, and the sound of it sent a strange feeling shafting through her. Nobody had ever spoken her name in quite that way before. 'Why not?' he asked her again. 'Cara's a lovely name. Be seeing you.'

Were his parting words a promise, or a threat? With her fingers pressed to her throbbing lips, Cara stumbled to the van door and watched him stride away.

Someone else watched him, as well. Out of the corner of her eye she saw the curtains of Linda's living-van dropping back into place as Tyler vanished into the darkness beyond the tent lights.

Slowly Cara closed her own door. Had Linda seen Tyler simply pass by, or had she actually seen him leave her own van? If she had, Cara did not doubt that Linda would make the utmost capital of it with Gio in the morning.

Hurriedly she donned a housecoat over her ring costume, and slipped back through the door, making for her uncle's van. She must let him know right away that Tyler had decided to allow the circus to remain in the Park. If she did not, she knew that both her aunt and her uncle would spend a sleepless night worrying about it.

She dared not let Mitcham Brook know the real reason for the reprieve. If she did, she knew her uncle's reaction would be swift, and angry. Before daylight, the circus would be packed up and already on the road, and if that happened they would lose all the rest of their winter bookings, and be faced with unimaginable difficulties trying to refund ticket money.

She hardly dared to think about the reason for their reprieve herself. Tyler was prepared to allow the circus to remain, if she was prepared to let him make love to her. It was blackmail of the very worst kind, and she felt sick as she hurried up the steps of her uncle's van.

She was not too surprised to find Gio already there when she walked through the door.

'It's all right, I've explained the situation to Gio,' Mitcham Brook said as she hesitated. 'I'm waiting for Lord Broadwater now. I felt sure he'd want to see me right after the show, but he hasn't come yet.'

'I've just seen him,' Cara announced baldly.

'What's he been doing all this time?' Gio exclaimed. 'It's ages since the show finished.'

'He's probably been prowling round the circus to make sure we've tucked all the animals in bed, and kissed them good night,' Cara said with a brave attempt at flippancy.

'Did he say anything about us having to move out of the Park?' her uncle interrupted her impatiently.

'Yes. He's changed his mind. He's letting us stay on.'

It was almost worth it to see the relief spread over her uncle's face at the news, Cara thought. Almost.

Gio's face did not reflect the same feelings. His expression was openly suspicious, and his next words made it clear that he had now discovered from Mitcham Brook who the real Lord Broadwater was.

'What did it take for you to make him change his mind?' he demanded angrily. 'Your make-up's all streaked . . .'

She had forgotten about her make-up. Dismayed, Cara raised a shielding hand to her cheeks. Tyler's kisses must have streaked them.

'I was just starting to cream off my make-up when he called to tell me,' she countered swiftly. 'I didn't stop to finish it, because I knew Uncle Mitch would want to know right away.'

'If you're lying . . .' Gio took a threatening step forward.

'That's quite enough of that, Gio.' Mitcham Brook half rose from his armchair, checking the trapeze man sternly. 'Apologise to Cara immediately,' he thundered.

'It may be Cara who needs to apologise.'

'Do as I say, or get out.' The circus owner's tone brooked no argument, and Gio flushed darkly.

'Oh, all right, I apologise,' he muttered ungraciously. 'But in my opinion it might not be a bad thing if we did move out of the Park after all.' And with that parting shot he slammed out of the van, leaving a loaded silence behind him.

Cara broke it. 'Thanks, Uncle Mitch. I needed a bit of support in that direction,' she said relievedly.

'I won't have Gio behaving in that way towards you,' her uncle frowned. 'If he gets out of hand again, let me know, and I'll cut him down to size.'

If he knew how Gio had already behaved towards her, he would carry out his threat and sack her partner on the spot, but Cara resisted the temptation to tell him. Whatever Gio's personal shortcomings in her eyes, he was a top-rank trapeze artist. They worked well together professionally, and their act topped the bill.

To have to replace him at short notice would involve a great deal of trouble, not only to find another artist of his calibre this late in the season, but to work up a routine together after being used to Gio for so long.

'I don't think he's likely to misbehave again, now you've spoken to him,' she placated, privately justifying her optimism with the thought that if Gio's temper did threaten to get the upper hand again, she could always cool it now by threatening to tell her uncle.

The smell of after-shave lotion greeted her when she returned to her van, lingering like a ghostly reminder of its wearer in the small mobile dwelling. Impatiently Cara flung open the window to clear the air, and sat down in front of her dressing-table to clean her face free of its ring make-up before she went to bed.

Her mirror showed her all too clearly the evidence that had inflamed Gio's suspicions. The heavy make-up made the streaks glaringly obvious, and with a muttered exclamation she pushed aside the bottle of cleansing lotion and pad of cotton wool, and jumped to her feet again, suddenly revolted by the garish colour.

Turning the taps to full flood she swiftly filled the washbasin and soaped and swilled with ruthless hands, and towelled her face afterwards to a pink glow in a vain attempt to rub away the feel of Tyler's kisses.

She returned to her dressing-table to inspect the results of her efforts in the mirror, almost, she thought with a derisive smile, as if she expected the marks of his kisses to show.

Her eyes widened as they met their own reflection, hugely dark, and brilliant with a light in them that she had never seen there before. They glowed with a strange inner excitement that sent the blood rushing through her veins, making her pulses race.

Far from feeling tired, as she usually did after the evening performance was over, she felt vividly alive, and sleep evaded her as she lay later in the darkness. In spite of the open window, the faint scent of after-shave lotion still remained, teasing her nostrils, and bringing back Tyler's face to haunt her each time she closed her eyes.

As she tossed and turned, the echo of his voice returned to mock her.

'There could be a real person underneath the make-up ... Cara's a lovely name ...'

The next morning, black smudges under her eyes betrayed her sleepless night, and after a stint grooming the horses Cara joined her partner in the big top for the usual early practice session.

Linda was already there, idly juggling with her clubs, close to the tent flap. Making sure she would not miss seeing her and Gio come in, Cara guessed shrewdly.

'I see you've taken to having late-night callers,' Linda called across maliciously when she caught sight of them. 'Who was he, or shouldn't I ask?'

'You're not telling Gio anything he doesn't already know,' Cara returned bluntly, neatly spiking the other girl's guns. 'In case you haven't already found out, my caller was Lord Broadwater, and Gio was in on the discussion with Uncle Mitch afterwards as to the reason for his visit, which doesn't concern you.'

Deliberately she elevated Gio to the position of her uncle's confidant, and watched contemptuously as he preened himself under her subtle flattery. It helped to sweeten his mood during the practice session, however, and as soon as it was over Cara joined her uncle and aunt for a late breakfast in the latter's van.

'Did Lord Broadwater say exactly what made him change his mind last night, and decide to allow us to stay on in the Park?' Mitcham Brook asked curiously, and Cara went still.

'He satisfied himself that we'd got no wild animals in the circus,' she answered cautiously, and pretended to be absorbed in eating her breakfast, to avoid having to look at him.

Nothing wild on *four legs.*

Her teeth gripped hard on her toast, biting on the mockery of Tyler's taunt.

'He gave us all a nerve-racking time, waiting for his decision,' her uncle said ruefully, as if he was satisfied by her explanation. 'Perhaps now he's satisfied himself on that score, he'll come and visit us again.'

It was nothing to what he had done to her own nerves, and Cara was certain he would visit again. And again. The only thing she was not sure of, was when.

'It's still early. I think I'll go and exercise Pride.'

Anything was better than waiting around, dreading Tyler's arrival. She shared the last of her toast with Pride, and the mare crunched happily on the accustomed titbit as she vaulted on to her back.

Deliberately she rode away from the Park, taking the lane instead that led towards the shore. Tyler had intimated that he rode in the Park himself each day, and the longer she could avoid another meeting with him, the better.

She despised herself for her cowardice as she rode on to the firm sands. Maybe it would have been better if she had remained at the circus after all, and confronted him, and shown him that she was not ready to submit meekly to his blackmail. At the circus there would have been other people around during the day, ready to back her up.

The shore was deserted.

Impatiently she touched her heels to the mare's sides,

and cantered along the edge of the receding tide.

Tyler's visit last night had left her feeling nervy and on edge, and she flew along the waterline as if by her very speed she could outdistance the thought of him, the memory of his arms holding her, his kisses on her lips.

The wind sang in her ears, and her hair streamed out behind her in a dark cloud. 'You'd make an excellent jockey,' Tyler called out, and guided the golden stallion to canter beside her.

'Where did you spring from?' Cara spun sharply on the mare's back, her eyes opening wide in mingled consternation and anger. 'I didn't hear you coming behind me.'

A revealing glance to the rear showed her a second row of horseshoe-shaped prints marking the wet sand, and running parallel with her own.

He must have seen her from the Park as she set out on her ride, and deliberately followed her all the way along the lane to the beach, tracking her, she realised angrily, as unobtrusively as he would track a creature he wanted to film, carefully keeping his victim unaware of his presence until he chose his own moment to reveal himself.

'At the pace you were setting, you wouldn't hear anything except the whistle of the wind.'

'I'm entitled to gallop on the beach if I want to. The shore belongs to everybody.'

Not exclusively to Tyler Moncrieffe, which meant he had no power to order her off it. The breeze and the exercise combined had whipped her cheeks to a rosy glow, unmarred this morning by make-up, which she did not use except when she was in the ring, and the feel of the mare under her gave her the confidence to defy him.

'If it's a gallop you want, I'll race you as far as the breakwater,' he challenged, and his teeth glinted white in a grin.

'You're on.'

She did not stop to think that she could not win, and she did not wait for his signal to start. With a swift touch of her heels she leaned over the mare's back, and gave Pride her head.

The pace was breathtaking, and sheer exhilaration swept away the last vestiges of Cara's jangled nerves. Neck-and-neck the two horses raced along the sands. Her experience in the Park told Cara that her mare had no hope of outdistancing the stallion, but her mind raced at the same tempo as the flying hooves, searching for a way to outwit its rider. Follow her, would he?

The breakwater loomed ahead, and Tyler drew in his galloping horse preparatory to turning. Cara grabbed her opportunity. Instead of following suit, she set Pride straight at the wooden barrier without slackening speed.

The spotted mare rose to the obstacle like a show-jumper, and galloped on, leaving Tyler behind her on the other side. She heard him shout, and laughed exultantly, and turned the mare at a sharp angle, making for the dunes, and the lane that she knew would meet them further along, and bring her back to the circus.

The soft sand of the dunes muffled any sound, and she risked a glance over her shoulder. Her ruse had not succeeded for long. With lightning reaction Tyler was already across the breakwater, and racing in her wake, pursuing her with a relentless determination that sent a strange thrill shafting through her that was almost akin to fear.

The lane loomed up, and she urged Pride to greater speed. The mare's hooves hammered on the iron surface, and an echo hammered behind them, gaining on her, and then he was racing alongside, his hand reaching down as it had in the Park to grasp at her rein. In the space of a few yards he brought both horses to a blowing halt.

'I won,' Cara panted triumphantly.

'You cheated.'

'All's fair in . . .' She stopped, her cheeks firing. What on earth had made her blurt out a thing like that?

'In love and war?' Tyler finished for her. 'Which is it to be between us, Cara? Love, or war?'

He moved the stallion tight in against her mount's side, so close that the highly polished leather of his riding-boot nudged against her leg. Hastily she kneed Pride away, the only few inches that were left between herself and the hedge, and instantly, like a dancer following its partner, Tyler moved the stallion across beside her.

Another nudge. Cara glared. 'Move over, you're crowding me,' she snapped, and flipped her leg up and tucked it behind her on the mare's back. For the first time in her life she regretted not using a saddle, which would have given her another inch or two of extra height, and done much for her rapidly oozing confidence.

'That will do nicely,' he said approvingly.

She divined his intention split seconds before he leaned over and plucked her off the mare's back, as neatly and easily as plucking a pea out of a pod, and by then it was too late.

She could have kicked herself at the ease with which he had manoeuvred her into the position he wanted. He must have seen her flip her leg behind her in the ring, and calculated that habit would make her do the same thing now if he crowded her closely enough.

If her leg had been in its proper place, she could have gripped her feet under the mare's belly and held on, but with only one leg it was an impossibility, and Tyler's triumphant grin knew it.

Cara went rigid as he drew her across his saddle, leaving her feet dangling helplessly above his boots.

'Put me down,' she yelled angrily. 'What do you think you're playing at?'

'What makes you think I'm playing?'

His tongue flicked the pale pink tip of her ear where it peeped through the dark curtain of hair, and the light, sensual touch drove her to frenzy.

'Put me down.'

Her rigid muscles exploded into a struggling armful, and the stallion shifted uneasily under the unseemly battle being waged upon its back.

'So, it's to be war?' he mocked her.

'Too right, it's war,' she shouted furiously. 'I loathe you.'

'If you don't keep still, you'll fall. There's no safety-net below you here.'

If she remained in his arms, she would need another kind of safety-net than the one she used in the ring.

The man was a high-handed, prejudiced, self-opinionated blackmailer, and she hated the sight of him. He was also dangerously attractive, and the woman in her was instinctively responding to those attractions. She hated herself for the ecstatic fingers of sensation that uncurled themselves inside her at his touch, in a way they never did when Gio held her.

'Loose me,' she panted desperately, and redoubled her efforts to escape his hold.

His laugh should have warned her, but she was too incensed to notice anything but the turmoil of her own feelings. 'If that's what you want,' he conceded, and relaxed his hold upon her. Her own frantic struggles did the rest.

'Help, I'm slipping.'

The metal road lay hard and unyielding underneath her, promising a painful landing, and possible injury, if she fell.

Her resistance vanished, and she wrapped her arms round the only security that offered itself, that of her captor's waist. 'You let me go on purpose,' she accused him furiously. 'You knew I'd slip.'

'You told me to.'

'I've changed my mind.'

'I knew you would, sooner or later.'

For an endless minute he allowed her to remain suspended, punishing her for fighting him, and then, with a triumphant laugh, he scooped her back up across his saddle, laying her across his lap so that her face was upturned close to his.

'You're despicable,' she spat, furiously.

Fear of falling forced her to lie still, but her eyes continued to fight him. Wide and black, they smouldered with the combined effects of fury and fright, and glared defiance up into his face that hovered unnervingly close above her own.

'And you're very lovely, *Cara mia*. Has no one ever told you?'

'Don't call me that. I'm not *your* Cara.'

A traitorous imp inside her wondered what it would be like to belong to him, wholly and completly. To lie in his arms, not for an endless minute on a bare, deserted beach, but for days, and nights for ever, because she belonged there.

'One day you'll belong to somebody.'

'Never.' Ruthlessly she quelled the imp. 'I'm my own person. I'll never belong to anybody but myself,' she declared fiercely.

'Don't fight your fate, Cara.'

With a lean index finger he traced the contours of her heart-shaped face, and she had to steel herself not to flinch away. His touch seemed to burn as if his finger-end was red hot, and would leave a weal across her soft flesh. 'You're too lovely to belong to yourself alone,' he chided her.

'I'll fight every inch of the way.'

'No man worth his salt relishes an easy conquest.'

He bent his head low over her, and her lips parted, her teeth gleaming in protest at what she knew must come next. It came with a surprising gentleness.

His lips teased apart the soft curves of her mouth, demanding a response, and yet careful not to hurt. She lay rigid in his arms, holding her breath, fighting a sudden inexplicable longing that flared inside her, as intense as a pain.

The touch of his lips, the feel of his hands holding her, was like an electric probe homing in on the pain, until it became an exquisite agony almost more than she could bear.

The quicker she turned off the current the better, before something exploded out of control, Cara thought, appalled, and began frantic efforts to pull herself upright on his lap.

'You taste nicer without make-up on.' His lips started a voyage of discovery across her cheeks.

'In that case I'll wear make-up all day, every day.'

'I'll just have to dig that much deeper to reach what's underneath.'

He was unstoppable. The pain was spreading, taking control. A low moan broke from her lips, and she made a convulsive movement in his arms, pulling herself upright. Pulling herself towards him, not away, she realised aghast.

'You perform very nicely out of the ring, as well as in it,' he grinned approvingly. 'With a little bit more practice . . .'

'I'm not looking for practice, least of all with you.' Cara scrubbed a fierce hand across her mouth, trying to rub away the feel of his kisses from her throbbing lips. 'I detest you,' she hissed furiously.

'So you've said before,' he grinned, completely unmoved. 'But we mustn't let it make you late for the afternoon performance. The show must go on,' he mocked.

His long fingers gripped her round the waist, and with an easy movement he lifted her from off his lap and dropped her back neatly into place on top of the mare.

Without giving Cara time to get settled in her seat he gave the mare a light spank that sent the animal galloping away along the lane. Taken by surprise, it was all Cara could do to remain to top, and she ground her teeth in helpless fury as his mocking taunt followed her flight,

'I'll be seeing you, *Cara mia*.'

CHAPTER FOUR

CARA was hard at work grooming the sweating mare when Gio joined her.

'You've run Pride into a lather this morning,' he observed, and his voice sharpened suspiciously. 'Did you meet anyone in the Park?'

'I didn't go into the Park this morning. I can't gallop there because of the cattle.' Cara continued to groom with fierce concentration. 'I took Pride to the shore instead. There's no one around on the beach at this time of the year, and I can let her have her head there.'

It was not a complete lie. She had tried to avoid meeting Tyler, and it was not her fault that she had not succeeded.

'I expected you back early to do a bit more practice on your back somersault. You need to, if you're not to risk another fall like last night,' Gio carped, and Cara said tightly,

'Our profession's full of risks.'

She had not expected them to include Tyler Moncrieffe. The tawny-haired naturalist had succeeded in upsetting her balance mentally as well as physically. The mere thought of him was enough to make her pulses pound, and she hated herself as well as him because of it.

'It isn't any use you hanging around waiting for me. I've still got the dogs to groom,' she told Gio.

'Tomorrow morning, then,' her partner gave in grudgingly.

'I've got to go into Broadwater tomorrow morning, to arrange places in the local school for Pepi's children.'

Perversely Cara felt glad that for once she could produce a foolproof excuse not to give in to Gio. Pepi and his wife spoke very little English, and as a member of the circus-owner's family it automatically fell to

59

Cara's lot to attend to such domestic matters, as Gio was well aware.

'I don't see why it always has to be you who does these things,' he grumbled.

'You'll just to have to accept that it is, and put up with it. The children are fluent enough, but they're too young to enrol themselves.' Cara was in no mood to mince words. 'I'll be back from Broadwater in good time before lunch tomorrow to put in some practice then,' she told him firmly. 'I'm going to get cleaned up as soon as I've finished the dogs, and then it'll be time to get ready for the afternoon performance. You can help me groom some of them if you like.'

Her offer had the expected result of sending Gio away, shoulders hunched sulkily, back towards the line of mobile vans, and after dispensing fuss and tit-bits all round to the frisky pack when she finished with them, Cara was about to follow him when Ben waylaid her.

'Will you do the lasso-dancing for Poppy this afternoon?' the clown asked her, and to Cara's concern his usual cheerful face was puckered with worry.

'Isn't Poppy well?'

'She's not feeling too good. She seems to have some sort of tummy upset, but it's been going on now for quite a time.'

'She ought to see a doctor,' Cara urged. 'I thought she seemed to be a bit off colour during the show yesterday.'

'I've arranged an appointment. I'm going with her after the show this afternoon.'

'Who's going to act as stooge to your clown?'

As Tyler said, the show must go on, and automatically Cara's mind latched on to the practical difficulties of being one performer short.

'Linda will fill in until Poppy's better.'

The cast and the audience were each depleted by one, Cara thought whimsically as Mitcham Brook announced the first act, and she entered the ring on Pride's back.

The ringside seats reserved for the holders of complimentary tickets were this afternoon filled by

children, and without Tyler's presence, all the tension of
the previous evening was gone. So, too, was the sparkle.

The pace did not seem to go with quite such a swing.
The spangles lacked their usual bright glitter, and
although she performed her three backward somersaults
with faultless precision that earned her thunderous
applause from the audience, Tyler was not there to
witness them, and the applause rang hollowly in her
unreceptive ears.

The slick perfection of their own act restored Gio's
good humour sufficiently for him to unbend and offer
her rare congratulations.

'You're back to your old form,' he told her
condescendingly.

'I was never off it,' she retorted, and bore her
bouquet out of the ring feeling none of the excitement
and the magic she usually experienced at the end of a
show. All that her lack-lustre eyes could see was the
sham of the paper roses, attractively wrapped in their
cellophane covering, lying in her arms.

When she emerged from her van the next morning,
something seemed to be different about the line-up of
vans round the back of the big top. Cara looked at it for a
minute or two with a puzzled frown, unable to decide
what it was, and then her eyes lighted on the large open
space, like a missing front tooth, where the clown's van
had previously stood beside the generator wagon.

The wagon was still there. But Ben's van was missing.

'Did you think we'd done a moonlight flit?' the clown
grinned, coming up to Cara from the opposite end of
the row of vans. 'I'm just on my way to attend to the
infernal machine now.'

'I wondered for a dreadful minute if you'd decided to
move out, because of Poppy,' Cara confessed.

'What, move away from Mitch's circus? Never!'
exclaimed Ben. 'I've shifted our van to the other end of
the line-up, that's all, where it's away from the noise of
the generator.'

'Is Poppy still not well?'

'Poppy's fine, now she knows what it is that's causing
the problem,' Ben responded cheerfully. 'What's more,

the babies are fine, too.'

'Babies? In the plural?' Cara exclaimed delightedly.

'Twins,' the father-to-be confirmed happily. 'That's why I've moved our van. We can't have the babies next to a noisy generator.'

Cara laughed out loud at his volte-face. 'Poppy's been on to you for long enough to do just that, though I must say it's a drastic method of getting her own way,' she chuckled.

'I'll start up the generator, and then go and let the others know our good news,' Ben smiled, and Cara felt an unexpected pang as she watched him walk away on his happy errand.

Babies. Someone else's babies. Circus babies.

The pang subsided a little, and resolutely she tackled her morning chores, then hurried to collect the three children from Pepi's van, and set off for the bus stop with his reluctant brood in tow.

'Don't try to run back to the circus before home time,' she warned the three, as she left them in the care of the headmistress. 'You'll never grow up to be real troupers if you run away from things you don't like.'

She was sorely in need of taking her own advice, she reflected wryly as she made her way to Broadwater's shopping-centre with her list of wants tucked in her pocket.

The prospect of a whole winter camped in Broadwater Park, with the unnerving certainty of frequent meetings with its owner always looming over her, made her want to run away and hide.

The three meetings she had had with him so far had made it abundantly clear that she was incapable of handling Tyler, and equally disturbing, since that morning's meeting on the shore, she no longer felt sure that she could handle herself.

The manager of Broadwater's largest department store provided a distraction from her thoughts that was not altogether welcome. He hurried to greet her, hand outstretched, as she walked through the big swing doors.

'Miss Varelli! We're so looking forward to your performance here in a fortnight's time. As a promotion for our sportswear department, I'm sure it'll be a huge success,' he gushed.

Cara sighed, and resigned herself to losing precious time from her planned shopping. 'I hope so,' she agreed politely. 'Although today I've just popped in to do some shopping.'

She hoped silently that the manager would take her hint and not keep her talking for too long, or any opportunity to do shopping would be irretrievably lost. The headmistress of the school had detained her for longer than she had anticipated, and there was less than an hour to go before she must catch the bus back to the circus if she were to redeem her promise to Gio to join him for practice before the afternoon performance.

'You agreed to be seen arriving in one of our brand-name track-suits,' the manager prattled on, happily unaware of her growing impatience. 'I've had a selection of different colours put aside ready for you to choose from.' Taking Cara's abstracted nod as encouragement he pressed on, 'Perhaps you'd like to try on some of them now?'

'It would be better if I had my partner with me, and we could both try on our track-suits together.' Cara made a last bid to get away. 'We need to use the combined trapeze act for your promotion, with both myself and my partner wearing your track-suits, as you're promoting men's as well as women's sportswear. We'll come in together tomorrow,' she promised, and hastily made her escape while an assistant came up to speak to the manager.

A glance at her watch told her she would have to forgo her shopping for that morning if she were to have any hope of catching her bus, and it was with mounting irritation that she battled her way through the crowd of shoppers towards the nearest exit.

'Oops, sorry!'

She was so intent upon getting out of the store herself, she did not see the man who was trying to come in through the heavy swing doors at the same time, until they swung inwards, and she collided full tilt into him.

His arms shot out and caught her, preventing the door from swinging back on to her, and as Cara struggled to regain her balance she became uneasily aware of two things.

His arms continued to hold her for long after it was strictly necessary. And the familiar faint pleasance of his after-shave lotion warned her who it was who held her in his arms, even before she looked up and saw his face.

'Well, well, what a coincidence,' Tyler said cheerfully.

'Is it a coincidence, or have you followed me again?' Cara snapped angrily.

'Perhaps it's a bit of one, and a bit of the other,' Tyler acknowledged, unabashed. 'You're out of breath,' he discovered with interest.

'I'm in a desperate hurry. The manager of the store kept me talking, and I'll have to run if I'm to catch the bus back to the circus.'

The rapid rise and fall of her breast was caused by the capricious behaviour of her pulse, and it had nothing to do with her haste, which was centred now, not on bus timetables, but on the urgent necessity to remove herself from Tyler's arms.

Surreptitiously she tried to prise them from about her waist, but although they seemed to hold her loosely, they were as immovable as steel girders. Trapped, she glanced helplessly round her. The entrance to the store was crowded, and unless she created a scene it was impossible to lever herself free.

Furiously, she was reduced to begging, 'Please let me go, or I'll miss my bus.'

'What's the hurry?' With his arms still circling her, he flicked back a spotless shirt-cuff and consulted his wristwatch. 'Your afternoon show isn't due to go on for some time yet.'

'Gio wants me back to practise with him.'

'And do you have to do as Gio tells you?'

'No, of course not, but . . .'

A glance along the street told her the bus was already on its way. If the traffic lights turned to green and let it through, she would never be able to cross the road in time through the stream of lunch hour traffic.

'For goodness' sake let me go, or I'll miss it,' she exploded in exasperation.

The traffic lights turned to green, and let the bus through.

'You can't dash across the road among all that traffic. You'll get yourself killed,' Tyler tut-tutted, and hung on to her.

In vain Cara wrenched at his fingers, trying to prise them loose. With mounting fury she watched the bus fill up at the stop, and start on its way.

'I've missed it,' she wailed, and turned on him wrathfully. 'It's your fault. You held on to me deliberately.'

'I'll give you lunch to make up.' He slanted her a downwards glance, anticipating her refusal. 'It's an hour's wait until the next bus.'

'Eating anything with you would choke me,' she blazed. 'In any case, I never eat before a performance. You can't swing upside down on a trapeze with a tummy full of food.'

'Sounds reasonable,' he acknowledged. 'We'll settle for coffee instead.'

'I don't want . . .'

'Stop fighting, Cara. At least call an armistice while you're drinking your coffee. You can't drink and argue at the same time.'

Without quite knowing how it happened, Cara found herself back inside the swing doors, and sitting down at a table in the coffee-bar on the other side, and Tyler was sliding a steaming cup towards her.

She glowered at it balefully. 'I can't imagine why you should want to stand me lunch, or even a cup of coffee, when you're so dead set against the circus.'

'Yours isn't a conventional circus,' he conceded loftily. 'It's more a group of strolling players.'

'Have you changed your mind?' she taunted. 'We use animals.'

'Domestic pets.' He used her own words against her. 'I checked on them before I came to your van. They're in superb condition.'

'You've got a cheek,' Cara exploded. 'Who gave you permission to inspect them?'

'I took it, for the sake of the animals. Seeing the care you give to them yourself, you can hardly argue with that.'

He had scored a point, but Cara's expression remainded mutinous. 'They still do tricks in the ring,' she pointed out perversely.

'My red setter does tricks, and so does the stallion, for that matter.' His lips relaxed in a slight smile. 'We all teach our pets tricks, and they enjoy showing them off, the same as children do. Wild animals are different.'

'It's a good job some circuses still have them.' Cara ignored his sudden granite look and ploughed on doggedly. 'Do you remember those elephants that were massacred, a few years ago?'

'Do I remember?' he ejaculated ferociously. 'It was in all the papers at the time. An entire herd was destroyed, just because they happened to get in the way of some footling development or other. We tried our utmost to stop it, but there was absolutely nothing we could do.'

'Not quite the entire herd,' Cara contradicted. 'The slaughter was stopped, by, would you believe, circus people,' she taunted. Tyler made as if to speak, and she hurried on. 'The troupe happened to be in the area at the time, and they abandoned their tour and stepped in to rescue those animals that weren't already killed.'

'I didn't see anything about it in the papers afterwards.' He sent her a look as if he did not believe her.

'It didn't get into the papers,' Cara told him, more quietly. 'The circus people deliberately kept it low-key, in the hope that the world-wide publicity given to slaughtering the herd would so inflame public opinion that it would stop any further attempts being made to do the same thing somewhere else. Thank goodness, in that respect it was successful. If they'd let it be known what they'd done, the newspaper articles would have latched on to the rescue, rather than the happening, and it wouldn't have been half so effective.'

'How many elephants were saved?'

'About a dozen in all, mostly cows, and one or two calves. Some of them had already been shot and wounded, and had to be nursed back to health afterwards.'

There was a wealth of pity in Cara's voice, and an answering flash, that might have been for the animals, or it might not, appeared for a moment in the man's eyes.

'What happened to them?'

'After the uproar had died down, and the wounded ones were fit to travel, they were all quietly shipped out of the country. Some came to the safari parks in England, and some went to the Continent, and the last I heard of them they'd all settled down well in their new homes.'

Tyler gave an expressive whistle. 'Shipping that number of elephants must have been enormously costly. Who paid?'

'The circus people, of course. Who else?' Cara replied simply.

He was silent as he sipped his coffee. Perhaps he still did not believe her. Cara gave a mental shrug. If he wanted to take the trouble, he had only got to phone round the safari parks to check up on her story. There were not so many of them as to make the task impossible.

'Another coffee?'

'No.'

His eyebrows kinked. 'Battle resumed?' he quizzed lightly.

'Yes. No. Not exactly.' She had been so absorbed in her story, she had forgotten, for the moment. She remembered, and stiffened against him. 'I really must go. I've missed practice, thanks to you,' she reminded him tartly. 'I mustn't miss out on the chores as well. We're one short, with the clown's wife not being well.'

'Anything serious?' Oddly, Tyler sounded as if he might be genuinely concerned, and Cara shot him a surprised look.

'She's expecting twins,' she said briefly.

'Now, that'll be something to celebrate. Two little clowns.'

'She's welcome.'

'Don't tell me an animal-lover doesn't like children?'

'I'd love the twins,' Cara confessed. 'But not the job of raising them in a mobile home that's always on the move. It's no fun, from the woman's point of view.'

'I see there's a rebel in the camp. I thought the circus was a way of life.'

'A way of life needn't necessarily mean a jail sentence.' Cara checked herself sharply. This was no way to talk to a man who was a confirmed circus-hater. Guilt reddened her cheeks at having unburdened her own secret doubts to an outsider. 'I'm going.' She got up from her seat abruptly. 'There'll be a queue.'

'I'll give you a lift back.'

'No thanks. The public transport is quite adequate.'

'I've got to go back home anyway, to finish a script. It's got to be in the hands of the producer by the day after tomorrow.' Tyler rose and went with her into the street, where he cast a calculating eye on the long queue lined up at the bus stop opposite the store. 'If you join that lot, you won't get on the first bus.'

'I must, or I'll be late for the performance.' Cara turned on him angrily. 'If you hadn't made me miss the one before . . .'

'I wouldn't be able to offer amends now, and run you back to the circus.'

He took her arm in a tight grip and steered her purposefully towards a sleek Jaguar car parked at a nearby meter.

'I don't want . . .'

'The needle's getting stuck,' he told her curtly, and deposited her in the passenger seat with the crisp injunction, 'Fasten your seat-belt. And don't say, I don't want, again. It happens to be law. Or do I have to do it for you?'

His threat galvanised Cara into action. The thought of his arm reaching across her for the seat-belt, possibly staying round her . . .

Surely not, in the middle of a busy main street? But

she could not be sure of anything, with this man. He was a master of the unexpected. Her mind cringed from the possibility, while an unsuspected something inside her opened out welcoming arms with an urgency that staggered her.

Hurriedly she clicked the seat-belt into place in the lock, and her eyes flew up to meet his as she felt his hand brush her own while he performed the same service for himself.

His look held her, a long, sardonic taunt that latched on to what she was thinking, and jeered at her lack of courage for not putting it to the test. Her breath came unevenly through set teeth, and she said jerkily, 'It's locked in.'

He smiled, then, a brief mocking tilt of his lips, and his fingers left the belt lock and keyed the engine into life, his eyes leaving her face to search the road ahead.

She watched him surreptitiously as he guided the big car unerringly through the tightly packed traffic. His hands on the wheel, their long tanned fingers lightly curling round the rim; his body, relaxed in indolent grace against the luxurious seat, his gaze alert and watchful as he steered unscathed through gaps that left only the width of the paintwork between vehicles, and had Cara closing her eyes for fear of a collision that never came.

'These narrow streets were built for horse traffic, not horse-power.'

His remark kept her silent until the town was left behind, and the car began to pick up speed along the country roads. It was like its owner, Cara reflected, finely tuned, and with a controlled power that was ready to burst into life at the flick of a finger.

'This is quicker than the bus,' he remarked conversationally when the traffic had been left behind. Cara did not answer, and he grinned. 'Still fighting?' His tone was a taunt. 'As a matter of fact, I wanted to talk to you.'

'*Talk* to me?' She shot him a disbelieving look. On the last two occasions they met, talking was the last thing he had in mind.

'True.' He read her look, and his grin flicked back, and then as suddenly disappeared. 'About Falabellas,' he informed her solemnly. 'I've always had a yen to breed them myself.'

'Then why didn't you?' Her tone gave him no encouragement. Not that he needed any, she thought caustically.

'Because I've never had a settled home before I inherited the Hall.' He slanted her an oblique look. 'We've got more in common than you'd believe, *Cara mia*.'

'Such as?' she asked tartly. The *mia* rankled.

'Such as always being on the move with a soldier father. Never being able to keep pets because of the upset of having to leave them behind when we moved on, which was frequently. Never having close friends, even, for the same reason, except of course within the barracks communities, which at best is a restricted sort of world.'

'It sounds just like the circus,' Cara was startled out of her silence to admit.

'Pretty much the same,' he nodded. 'Like I said, we've got a lot in common. Seeing your uncle's herd of miniature ponies the other night revived a childhood longing. We can't leave all the conservation efforts to the circus people,' he said, deadpan.

'No one's standing in your way,' Cara returned acidly.

'Then perhaps you'll mention to your uncle that I'd like to have a word with him some time about breeding miniatures.' Taking her consent for granted—arrogantly, she fumed—he shot a sideways look at her unresponsive face, and his grin returned. 'I do have other longings, too. Strictly grown-up ones.'

So did she, Cara thought raggedly. Unsuspected ones, so far as she was concerned, until she met Tyler. She felt her cheeks redden, and saw with relief the gates of the Park looming ahead. She said hurriedly, 'Put me down at the gates. They'll be near enough. I can walk the rest of the way to my van.'

'I wouldn't be so churlish. I said I'd bring you home,

and I'll do just that.' He nosed the car carefully through the line of living-vans, and stopped in front of her own. 'Home,' he announced grandly.

'Thanks for nothing.'

Out of the corner of her eye, Cara espied Gio coming out of the big top. He would be furious because she had not turned up for practice, and the last thing she wanted was Tyler's presence to add fuel to the fire. Hurriedly she unlocked her seat-belt and grabbed for the door handle, and her fingers fumbled in her haste.

'Let me undo it for you.'

Tyler leaned across her, reaching slim fingers for the door handle. His arm trapped her in her seat more effectively than the belt. The move brought his face right opposite to her own, and he turned his head. Cara sucked in a difficult breath. Through the rear-view mirror she glimpsed Gio, turning towards them and knew he could not have missed seeing the car, and herself inside it. Knew Tyler must have seen Gio.

'If you won't thank me, I'll thank you, for coming with me.'

Twin devils of mischief lit Tyler's eyes, and before Cara could protest, 'You gave me no option,' he leaned closer and silenced the words with his lips. 'Thank you, *Cara mia*. Give my regards to Gio,' he mocked, and opened the door.

Cara ejected out of the car, and spun to face him. 'You . . .' she began furiously, only to be met by the soft thud of the door closing in her face. 'See you,' Tyler mouthed through the window, and with a wave of his hand he started the engine, and was gone.

'You've been with Broadwater.' Gio ran up, scowling after the departing Jaguar. 'I might have known it, when you didn't turn up for practice as you promised. I warned you, Cara. I saw him mauling you.'

'And Uncle Mitch warned *you*!' Cara rounded on Gio, her anger against Tyler spilling over on to her partner. 'Don't raise your voice to me, I won't put up with it. And as for Lord Broadwater mauling me, you want your eyes tested.' She leaned on the hope that Gio had been too far away to see what actually happened through the low back window of the car, and was merely voicing his own suspicions. 'All that he did was to reach across me to open the car door, because I couldn't manage the handle myself,' she lied.

Her unexpected attack silenced her partner momentarily, and Cara pressed her advantage before he had an opportunity to speak.

'If Lord Broadwater hadn't given me a lift back, I shouldn't have made it in time for the afternoon performance, let alone for practice. The manager of the store kept me talking for so long, I didn't even have time to do my shopping afterwards, and there was a queue a mile long for the bus.'

That at least was the truth, and it added a convincing ring to her voice that, she saw thankfully, made her partner hesitate.

'I thought all the details of our booking at the store were already finalised,' Gio muttered.

'The manager wanted to go over them again to make sure he hadn't forgotten anything. Oh, and I promised we'd go in together tomorrow to try on our track-suits. He wanted me to try mine on this morning, but I thought it would be better if we did it together, because I didn't know if you'd want our colours to match, or contrast,' Cara finished slyly.

It was prudent to cool Gio down before they went in the ring together, in case his temper got the upper hand, and he forgot Uncle Mitch's warning. Cara's exasperation against Tyler increased. What was a moment's amusement for him could have unpleasant consequences for herself.

'Match,' Gio was saying, clearly mollified that she had deferred to his wishes in respect of the track-suits. 'We'll go in first thing, and spend the morning in Broadwater together.'

To her relief he made no further reference to the subject during the performance, which went off without a hitch. She swung on the trapeze with faultless precision that gave Gio no possible cause to complain, and her routine on the high wire passed perfectly.

But for Cara, the thrill was gone. Mechanically she

worked her way through the routines, and for the first time ever she found them a chore, and when the performance was over, she felt weary and drained.

She fed Pride and the ponies, and escaped back to her van to change. She flinched as her lack-lustre eyes stared back at her from the mirror, seeing the garish ring make-up. She also saw beyond it, to a future that consisted of nothing but an endless repetition of the same thing, a prospect that filled her with growing aversion and dismay.

Her sense of guilt deepened at finding that the reservations about circus life which she had confided to Tyler widened to include her work.

The next morning she slipped a couple of tablets into her mouth under cover of her usual after-practice cup of coffee in her uncle's van, to ease the throbbing headache she had woken up with.

'The pace will ease off a bit when we close the big top, and start on the private bookings,' her uncle consoled her. His keen look had caught her movement, and attributed the dark shadows under Cara's eyes to entirely the wrong reason.

'I'll be glad of a bit of peace and quiet for a change,' Cara confessed, aware that the effects of her restless night must show on her face, and anxious to stem any awkward questions from her aunt and uncle.

'There won't be much peace and quiet round here for the next few days,' Beth Brook said ruefully. 'The fairground people moved on to the common last night.'

Cara grimaced into the hollow privacy of her coffee mug. Normally she enjoyed the carnival atmosphere the fairs brought with them. Whenever the circus worked for more than a few days in one place, one or other of the fairs usually came to camp nearby, each benefiting from the spin-off trade from the other.

Cara liked the fairground people. Their profession, like that of the circus, usually ran in families, and she knew them all, and looked forward to renewing acquaintanceships whenever their paths crossed, but to her overstretched nerves the prospect of the added noise was less than welcome.

'Gio and I are taking Pepi's children to school, and then we're going on to the store to try on our track-suits this morning,' she told her aunt. 'Is there anything you need while we're in Broadwater?'

'I've only got a few letters to post.'

Cara tucked them into her pocket, and grasped the two eldest children by the hand, while Gio hoisted the youngest one to his shoulders as they walked together to the bus stop. He was in a good mood this morning, playing with the children. Playing to the gallery, Cara thought cynically, wanting to impress her with the ease with which he slipped into a domestic role.

'Be good,' she bade the children automatically as she left them at the door of the school, and watched a bleak picture of herself saying the same thing to her own and Gio's children in a few years time, if she allowed her partner's persistence to wear her down, and finally gave in and married him out of sheer loneliness and despair.

'The Post Office is over there if you want to get rid of your letters,' Gio said as they reached the shopping-centre.

'That's a good idea.'

Cara delved into her pocket for the envelopes. She stepped towards the curb, ready to cross the road, when her eyes lit on a familiar tawny mane ducking under the low lintel of the Post Office doorway.

Tyler must have come in to post his script, and Cara pulled back on to the pavement hurriedly. He was the last person she wanted to meet while she was with Gio. Knowing her partner's jealous temper, at best it might provoke an embarrassing scene. At worst, it might rebound on herself during the afternoon performance, and in spite of Uncle Mitch's warning to Gio, it was something Cara did not feel inclined to risk.

So far, her partner did not appear to have seen the other man. 'There's a pillar-box along the street on this side. It'll save us from having to cross the road in all this traffic,' she said hastily.

Quick as a thought she grasped Gio by the arm, and almost ran him along the street towards the red box. A quick sideways look showed her Tyler standing on the edge of the curb looking in their direction, and she pushed the letters through the iron slit and turned Gio towards the nearest shop window.

'Let's have a look in here for a minute,' she urged. 'I don't know what to get Aunt Beth for Christmas.'

Nothing was further from her mind than Christmas shopping, but with her back towards Tyler she felt less conspicuous, and she glued her nose to the plate-glass window. It was a jeweller's shop, she saw thankfully, which at least gave credence to her excuse for wanting to look at its wares.

'There may be some brooches in the window on this side,' she suggested.

She plucked at Gio's sleeve. The display they were looking at, Cara saw nervily, was backed by bright mirror glass, giving a view from both sides of the serried trays of rings on display. And a perfect view of the Post Office forecourt on the other side of the street.

She could see Tyler clearly, still standing waiting on the edge of the pavement. His reflection was as clear as if he were standing beside her, and, she realised with growing panic, he could not miss seeing her when the traffic lights turned to red and stopped the flow of cars for long enough to enable him to cross on to the pavement on their side. What would be more natural than for him to come across and speak to her, and precipitate the very explosion she was most anxious to avoid?

'Let's go inside,' she urged Gio. 'They might have more choice in there.'

The inside of the shop offered her only refuge, and urgently she pulled her partner with her through the door. Gio came, nothing loath, with a hopeful, 'I saw some nice engagement rings in the window, that aren't too dear.'

Cara disregarded him. She squinted back through the window to check where Tyler had got to. He was already halfway across the street, she saw, but now he was joined by two other men, and they were talking together.

One was Daniels, the man she had seen at the Hall,

but she did not recognise the other. It did not matter. Tyler was unlikely to leave his companions to join her now, even if he saw her. She went weak with relief, and turned her attention to a tray of brooches which the assistant put on the counter for her to inspect.

'This silver-mounted coral will do nicely,' she decided.

She lingered long enough over her purchase to give the three men ample time to get away, before she turned to the shop door. Gio lingered beside a tray of rings. 'These solitaires are reasonably priced,' he said.

'Buy one to fit Linda,' Cara said shortly, and in a fit of remorse restored his good humour later by meekly accepting a bright scarlet track-suit to match his own preference.

'An excellent choice,' the store manager enthused. 'You'll both be clearly seen in bright colours.'

Privately, Cara thought they would stand out in a fog, and she chivvied Gio back to the bus, fobbing off his grumbles with the excuse, 'It's too crowded to go shop-gazing in comfort. Let's get back early. I want to put in some extra practice to make up for the time I lost yesterday.'

She made it sound as if the loss was a personal disaster, and to prove it she drove herself and her partner to the limit when they returned, trying by sheer effort to make up for her disturbing lack of enthusiasm, which she discovered had still not returned after a night's rest, as she told herself hopefully the day before that it must.

'The fairground sounds as if it's doing good business,' Gio commented as the music from the roundabouts hit them with full force when at last they emerged from the big top.

'I could do without the noise they're making,' Cara complained, and seeing her partner's surprise added, 'I've got a headache. It's battling through the shopping crowds this morning, I expect. I'll go and lie down for a bit. Perhaps it'll go.'

She gave Gio a wan smile to underline her need to be

left in peace, and to her relief he accepted her plea and let her go without argument.

Alone in her van, her restless mind denied her the peace she sought. A jumble of mixed emotions that refused to sort themselves into any kind of coherent order made her pace up and down the van, until at last in desperation she ducked under the shower, as if the force of water would wash them away.

Tyler ... the circus ... Tyler ... Gio ... Tyler. The thoughts ran round and round in her head like a caged hamster on an exercise wheel, and she pulled on jeans and a sweater and began to brush her hair with savage strokes, trying to straighten her mind into submission in the same way she straightened the shining strands of her hair.

'Confound the man, can't he even leave me in peace in the privacy of my own van,' she muttered angrily.

'Cara, we've got a visitor.'

Cara was just about to put down the brush in despair when her aunt's voice called her from the next van, and she jumped to her feet with a sigh of relief.

It would be one of the fairground people, come to catch up on the news, she guessed. Just the thing to stop her mind from thinking. Forgetting her headache, and her desire to lie down, she ran eagerly up the steps of the next-door van.

'Hello, how are . . .?'

The greeting died on her lips, and she stood stock-still and stared as Tyler rose from the couch at her entrance.

'He's come to have another look at the Falabellas,' her uncle said.

'And he's staying to see the show this afternoon,' her aunt added in a pleased voice.

CHAPTER FIVE

'YOU'VE seen the show once. Why do you want to see it again? We haven't imported any wild animals in the meantime,' Cara said acidly.

'Cara!' her aunt expostulated.

Resolutely, Cara steeled herself against Beth's protest, and kept her eyes fixed on Tyler. His tawny stare returned the compliment, appraising her coolly from her sleekly groomed head to the tips of her fingers, and her colour rose. With an effort she kept her hands from clenching with the tension that screamed inside her, and she met him look for look and insisted, 'Why?'

'Tyler's giving us a private booking,' her uncle said with a warning frown.

'*You?* A private booking?'

Cara's eyes rounded in undisguised astonishment, as much at Mitch's surprising use of their visitor's first name as at the unexpected information.

'Traditionally there's a party held at the Hall each Christmas, for the estate children,' Tyler answered her evenly. 'It would be useful to have selected acts from your show to entertain them. I understand you take private bookings.'

She had told him so himself, and Cara could have kicked herself now for doing so, but never in her wildest dreams did she imagine that Tyler might become a client.

'So you're prepared to put aside your prejudices against the circus when it suits you?' she said sweetly, and saw Tyler's face tighten.

'I think I've acknowledged this isn't a conventional circus,' he returned stiffly.

'But you've already seen one performance. Surely you can remember the acts without seeing them again?'

'I watched the previous show with a different purpose

78

in mind,' he reminded her. 'This time, I shall decide which acts will be most suitable for a children's party.'

Would he decide upon her own act?

The question quivered like summer lightning in the air between them. His eyes held her own, and an enigmatic smile played at the corners of his lips.

Anger flared up in Cara as she watched him. He was playing with her, cat-and-mouse. Waiting for her to ask if he wanted her act, so that he could refuse, and humiliate her. Well, if that was what he wanted, she would not give him the satisfaction, she fumed.

With an independent toss of her head she said, 'The department stores have got room, but I don't think a private house . . .'

She shrugged, and allowed the doubt to hang along with the question, her manner dismissing any possible bookings to the realms of a juggler or a clown, but emphatically nothing that required large apparatus.

She was aware that she was being perverse, putting off a possible customer, and she could feel the surprise and disapproval of Mitch and Beth clear across the van, but she could not help herself.

The question, would he choose herself? hammered at her mind with dreadful persistence, and the tension of not knowing, and having to await Tyler's pleasure to find out, rasped at her already taut nerves, and in self-defence she took the only course open to her, to make sure he had no opportunity to either choose or reject her.

'There won't be sufficient space for the large apparatus acts in a private house,' she told him flatly.

'There'll be plenty of room in the big hall,' he disagreed immediately. 'It's divided by a screen in the centre, and when that's thrown back it's a full-sized ballroom. The only difference will be that the performing area will be oblong, instead of circular, and, of course, it's parquet floor, not sawdust or turf. Why not come to the Hall and check it out for yourself?' he challenged, when Cara remained silent.

'That's an excellent idea.' Mitcham Brook gave her no opportunity to refuse. 'Cara always goes along to check the space available for private bookings anyhow, just in case there might be difficulties.'

Her difficulty was not the ballroom at the Hall, but its owner, Cara thought raggedly. Between her uncle and Tyler she was trapped, and it was her own fault for trying to put obstacles in Tyler's way. She might have known he would find some way to out-manoeuvre her, she realised bitterly.

'I can't stop to discuss it now. I've got to go and harness Pride and the ponies, ready for the ring.' She used the only escape-route left to her, and made for the door.

'Why not go along with her, Tyler?' Unwittingly Mitcham Brook once again foiled her, with the amiable invitation to his guest. 'You can look the ponies over, and see if they're what you have in mind.'

'Surely you're not thinking of *selling* him the miniatures?'

Shock snubbed Cara to a halt in the doorway of the van. It was impossible to imagine Mitcham Brook without his herd of miniature ponies, but in her present insecure mood she felt that anything was possible, and her face was a study in perplexity as she waited for his answer.

Her uncle laughed at her expression. 'Of course not,' he scoffed, 'but it's sensible for Tyler to have a look at my ponies before he starts a herd of his own. He'll be able to run a good-sized herd in the Park,' he went on, with a faint trace of envy in his voice. 'He'll be able to go into the business of selective breeding on a much larger scale than I'm able to.'

'Quality is better than size,' Cara retorted waspishly, and she scowled as she led the way reluctantly towards the ponies.

The private bookings for the party, and now the shared interest with her uncle in the Falabellas, would provide Tyler with the perfect excuse for frequent visits right into the heart of the circus camp.

If he would bother to make excuses, which she doubted, and wondered broodingly whether his interest in the Falabellas was genuine, or a calculated ploy to give him access, because he knew the miniature ponies were in Cara's charge.

Whatever the reason, there would be no way now she could avoid him, and Cara wondered uneasily how her already embattled senses would respond to such close contact. Simply walking beside him made her tingle with awareness, and to combat it she said sharply,

'The stallion kicks.'

Uncharitably she hoped the frisky little miniature would demonstrate its vice, but to her chagrin the animal for once controlled its high spirits, and trotted up to them docilely along with the mares.

'He's a beautiful little creature.'

Tyler whistled softly, and reached out his hand, and to Cara's amazement the little stallion allowed the stroking fingers to caress its head and neck, a familiarity it previously accorded to no one except herself and her uncle.

The hairs on her own nape began to prickle, as if the hands might be stroking her own dark head instead of that of the pony, and shocked at the sensation, which was so strong as to be almost real, she turned away swiftly to reach for the harness to hide the hot tide of colour that flooded her cheeks.

When she turned back, Tyler was digging deep into the pocket of his well-cut tweeds, and offering something to the stallion that tempted it to eat out of his hand.

'Don't feed him before he goes in the ring, or the titbits I give to him won't have any effect,' she snapped.

'Bribes,' Tyler jibed, but he withdrew his hand nevertheless. Not, Cara suspected vexedly, because she had asked him to, but most probably because he had no more titbits in his pocket to offer.

'They're not bribes. They're rewards for good behaviour,' she contradicted him forcefully. 'Pass him on to me, so that I can fit on his harness and plumes.'

The little stallion baulked, wanting to remain and be fondled by the man, and Cara's irritation increased as she struggled to harness the animal while Tyler looked on.

Because he watched her, her fingers fumbled with the straps, and the pony began to fidget restlessly under her longer-than-usual ministrations, until she bade it impatiently, 'For goodness' sake, stand still, or I'll never get you all done in time.'

'I'll help you.' Tyler reached out and unhooked two of the small harness sets from the nearby rack. 'Which one goes on which pony?'

He seemed to know by instinct that each animal would have its own individual harness, tailor-made for the maximum comfort in the softest leather, and in desperation Cara bit back the curt refusal that sprang to her lips, and indicated with a wave of her hand the two ponies in question.

With a speed that surprised her, he kitted up the two, and turned to help her with the others, and soon all the eight miniatures were ready for the ring, nodding and tossing their heads with the vanity of children, to show off their bright plumes to this interested stranger.

'Behave yourselves while I do Pride.' Hastily Cara distributed eight pieces of apple among them, and gave a quick glance at her watch.

'We'll work together on the mare. It'll save time,' Tyler said.

He did not wait for Cara to assent, but began to strap and buckle as if he had been harnessing circus horses all his life, co-ordinating his movements easily to match her own.

It gave her a strange feeling to work alongside him. Now and then his hand on the harness encountered her own, and electric thrills shot through her at his touch, but she dared not pull away because the mare had to be harnessed, and time was swiftly running out.

She gritted her teeth, and forced herself to keep working. If this was going to be the pattern of the next few months, somehow she would have to steel herself to endure it if she were to have any hope of surviving unscathed.

The mare done, she fled to her van to put on her own costume and make-up, and vaulted agilely on to Pride's back just in time as Mitcham Brook's whistle shrilled its warning to the performers to get into line.

She pretended not to see Tyler's outstretched hand, held up courteously to help her to mount. She shrank from any further contact with him, nervily conscious that his presence in the audience would prove distraction enough during the coming performance.

She wondered uneasily what Gio would make of Tyler coming to see another show. It was too much to hope that her partner would not notice. Nothing could be kept secret for long in a circus.

It would be best if she told him the reason herself, she decided cautiously, so that Gio would not be able to draw his own colourful conclusions, and take it out on her.

Cara signalled the miniature ponies into line behind her, and called over her shoulder to Tyler, 'You'll miss your seat at the ringside if you don't go right away.'

She did not look round to see if he had gone as she pressed her heels to the mare's side, and joined the line-up at the ring entrance.

'What's Broadwater doing here again?' Gio began belligerently, and visibly relaxed when she explained, and finished with an indifferent, 'It needn't bother us. He'll only want a juggler, or a clown, or something of that sort for a children's party.'

The music played its preliminary fanfare. Her uncle's voice rose to announce the first act, and saved Cara from any further conversation with Gio, and she rose gracefully to her feet on the mare's back as Pride cleared the ring entrance, and carried her in front of the packed audience.

And she knew, in that single, joyous moment, that all the former magic was back.

It spilled out like sunshine from the audience, giving the tinsel an added sparkle, and striking sparks of light from the sequins, and a feeling of inexplicable *joie de vivre* made Cara turn an unscheduled somersault on Pride's back.

Suddenly, she felt wonderfully, vitally alive, with a pulsing excitement that radiated from her like a tangible aura, and inspired her performance to a peak of perfection she knew she had never achieved before.

And all because Tyler sat at the ringside, watching her. Choosing the acts he would need for his children's party at Christmas. His tawny head drew her eyes like a magnet.

Would he choose her?

Cara despised herself for even thinking about it, but the question buzzed in her mind throughout the performance like a persistent mosquito, and refused to go away. And then the die was cast. The performance came to an end, and whatever choice Tyler had made from the various acts, the knowledge galled her that she would have to await his pleasure to find out.

The music rose to a peak as the performers filled the ring and took their final bows, and her bouquet sailed out from the audience and landed lightly in the sawdust at Mitcham Brook's feet. A single rosebud spilled beside it.

Cara's quick eye caught sight of the bud, and she made a mental note to repair the bouquet before the evening performance. The wire holding it must have snapped. She reached down and took the bouquet from her uncle, and her fingers automatically searched for the tear in the cellophane wrapping that had allowed the bud to escape.

Mitcham Brook held up the rose, and she took that from him, too. She would need it later to put back in its place among the other paper flowers.

'It's a real rose!' she exclaimed in surprise, as her uncle loosed it into her hand.

A waft of heady perfume was her first intimation that the bud had not escaped from her bouquet. It lay in her hand, and she stared down at it, startled. The petals were just beginning to open, flushed deeply pink on the inside, palely cream underneath, and she saw at once that it was not a florist's rose.

This bud had been recently plucked from a growing bush, late blooming in the unusually mild air. The clean, diagonal cut made by a pair of sharp secateurs still showed white at the bottom of the stem, and the distilled essence of lingering summer wafted round her like a message.

Instinctively her eyes flew to the ringside. Tyler sat impassive in his seat, watching her, giving her no indication whether or not it was he who had thrown the bud.

In her mind's eye she could visualise his doing so, his lean, tanned fingers holding the stem, waiting for the exact moment to toss the bloom, to land on precisely the spot he intended, making sure that the ringmaster would pick it up and hand it straight to her.

But she could not be sure. She had not actually seen Tyler throw it, which in the confusion of movement in the ring was hardly surprising. And it was something she could not question him about, in case he was not the donor.

If he was, like his choice of acts for the children's party, it was something she would have to wait for Tyler's pleasure to tell her or not, as he chose.

Dimly Cara was aware of the curious glances of the other performers. Of Gio's scowl, and her uncle's enquiring look, but they failed to make any impact. The warm, rich perfume of the rose wafted round her, insulating her from them.

The familiar dry, musty smell of the sawdust pervaded the ring, and compared to the rich velvet bloom on the pink petals in her hand, the paper roses her aunt had made with such care were brittle and lifeless. A sham, which was the way Tyler had described them, with undisguised scorn.

'Who's your secret admirer, Cara?'

'You're a dark horse, keeping it to yourself.'

The smile felt stiff on Cara's lips as she ran the gauntlet of good-natured teasing that was inevitable among the closely knit troupe.

'Is there a message with it?' Linda wanted to know in a brittle voice.

'There's no message.'

If it did come from Tyler, and it bore any message at all, it could only be in the nature of a taunt. Decrying, by contrast, the artificial flowers in her bouquet. And reminding her, by its perfume after he had gone, that he would be back again . . .

With her uncle's blessing, too. Cara gave a grimace of disgust. Tyler's grip on the circus was spreading like the tentacles of an octopus. He not only owned the land they camped on, he was now a client, and had ingratiated himself cunningly with Uncle Mitch by his interest, real or feigned, in the Falabellas.

With a spurt of anger, Cara longed to throw the rosebud down into the ring, and knee Pride forward to trample it underfoot, and reduce it to nothingness in the sawdust.

It would proclaim in a gesture her opinion of the rose, and its giver. She did not seriously question that it must be Tyler who had thrown the bud into the ring. Only he would have the subtlety to turn a flower into a dagger.

She raised her hand with the rose clutched in her fingers, but when she looked at the ringside seat it was empty. Its occupant was gone, along with the rest of the departed audience.

With a neat checkmate his absence rendered her gesture pointless, and if she merely threw the bud away, someone would be bound to notice, and it would cause more comment, and more questions.

'Cara.' Gio was moving towards her, and his scowl asked a question which she did not want to listen to, and could not answer.

'I can't stop now,' she called back.

Ruthlessly she pushed Pride through the crowd of performers at the ring entrance, and out into the blessedly cool air outside the tent, where she knew Gio could not follow her for some time, since he would be occupied in helping the other men with the apparatus, which meant she could avoid the pending scene which she knew resignedly was bound to come.

If she hurried, she could escape to the crowds in the fairground before Gio finished his chores, where if she were lucky he would not be able to track her down until it was time for the next performance.

Hastily she attended to Pride and the ponies, then fled to her van to change out of her ring costume. She flung the rose bud on to her bed along with her bouquet, showered, and slid into slacks and her favourite black sweater.

With fingers that were trembling she undid her hair from its topknot, and brushed it loose and free in deep, shining waves to her shoulders, working feverishly to banish the sweet, insidious perfume of the rose that hammered at the door of her resisting senses.

She did not care whether Tyler had chosen her to perform at his wretched party or not. She hoped he had not. She did not want any part of it, or of him. She picked up the rose, to throw it into the waste-bin.

The wood was hard and springy; the sharp end of it cut into her palm, and the pain forced her to loosen her grip, allowing the bud to slid further down into her hand. Unlike the stem, the petals were soft and yielding, pleading with her to hold them gently.

It was not the fault of the rose. Cara's fingers stroked the velvet head, and sudden compassion made their touch light and tender. It was not fair to vent her anger on the bloom. It was only an innocent emissary, and if it were not put into water very soon it would begin to droop.

Cara's love of flowers undermined her, and she looked round for a container, and the irony of it struck her as she searched that the first cut flower she had had in her van for months should be Tyler's rose.

Cut flowers were a luxury in a mobile home that was constantly on the move, with the inevitable risk of spillage from unstable vases, and the only container immediately available was her plastic toothbrush mug. Cara jettisoned the contents and filled it with water, and stood it on her dressing table with the rose inside.

The presence of the bud in her van might even help her, she decided wryly. While it lasted, the perfume from it would be a constant reminder to her to be on her guard against Tyler.

She slammed the door on its fragrance, and called out as she reached the next caravan, 'I'm going to have a look round the fair, to see if there's anything new since we saw them last.'

'I'll come with you as far as the Wallaces' van.' Her aunt joined her at the bottom of the steps. 'I promised Mrs Wallace I'd pop in and catch up with her news some time. Come with me,' Beth invited amiably.

Cara refused hastily. 'Not today. You know how Mrs Wallace talks, and I want to get a breath of fresh air before tonight's performance.'

'In that case, go along with Tyler,' her uncle's voice suggested, and Cara spun round with a muffled exclamation of dismay. She had not heard the two men approach across the soft turf, and it was too late to try to back out now, since Mitcham Brook must have heard what she said.

'I was just suggesting to Tyler that he should look at the sideshows at the fair, before he finally makes up his mind about which acts he wants for his children's party,' the circus-owner went on. 'Children like to be active, and it would be nice for them to have a coconut-shy, or something similar, as well as just something to sit and look on at.'

'It would be a nice idea to turn the whole party into a fair,' Beth suggested. 'It would be something different, and Father Christmas would fit in just the same, so far as the children are concerned. What do you think, Tyler?'

Cara did not care what he thought. He could turn his party into a full-scale musical comedy for all she cared, she thought mutinously, so long as she herself was not involved.

'It would make a change from playing ring o' roses,' Tyler smiled, and looked straight across at Cara as he said it.

So it *was* Tyler who had thrown the rose. Cara met his look with one of pure dislike. The silent image of the pink-and-cream bud lay like a gauntlet thrown down between them, and the light of battle flashed in Cara's eyes, taking up his challenge, and tossing it back scornfully.

Let him come to the circus as often as he liked. He could haunt it, if he wanted to, she would let him see it made not a whit of difference to her. And as for going with him round the fairground, the crowds would provide her with an adequate chaperone.

'It would be sensible if you looked at the sideshows together,' her uncle went on, following up his train of thought and happily oblivious of the silent thrust and parry taking place beside him. 'Cara has to come and check the room where you're holding the party, and if you tell her what you have in mind, you can discuss the possibilities together.'

'Once you've made up your mind what you want for your party, it shouldn't take long to work out a feasible plan,' Cara said crushingly.

Since she had been inveigled into helping with the organisation, she would see to it that the conversation was kept along strictly business lines, and conducted in the briefest time possible.

Her pride refused to allow her to ask Tyler which acts he had chosen from the performance this afternoon. Let him take as long as he wanted to tell her. She would show absolutely no interest in his choice beyond a purely impersonal, business one.

'I'll see Aunt Beth to Mrs Wallace's van first, then we can go and inspect the sideshows,' she said briskly. 'Uncle Mitch's suggestion of a coconut-shy is a good one.'

Business could be a useful armour, she discovered. It helped her to withstand the long, lean length of him strolling at her side, the occasional brush of his sleeve against her arm when he moved closer in as they picked their way through the crowds.

'We could use big, brightly coloured balls, instead of coconuts.' Tyler caught up the thread of their conversation again when they came to a welcome gap in the throng of fairgoers. 'Coconuts are a bit small for little children to be able to hit, but they'd manage with something the size of a kicking ball, and perhaps tennis balls to throw with.'

Cara sent him a surprised look. She had not expected such a depth of understanding from a bachelor. It pointed to a liking for children that his next remark confirmed.

'If we have a competitive game like a coconut-shy, there mustn't be any losers,' he went on adamantly. 'All the children must go home with a prize each, even the littlest ones, as well as their present from Father Christmas. I don't want tears of disappointment to mar their Christmas party,' he finished with an odd touch of wistfulness.'

'Considerate of you,' Cara remarked drily, and he answered with a reminiscent smile;

'I remember going to a party myself, when I was little, and being the only one whose balloon burst as we were about to come home. There weren't any more balloons left, so they gave me a cracker to make up, but I wanted a balloon the same as the others, and I yelled all the way home.'

'You must have been an absolute little horror,' Cara returned sweetly, and tried to ignore the peculiar feeling that shafted through her, at the thought of a small, tawny-haired boy in tears.

Ruthlessly she sent it packing with an offhand, 'There must have been plenty of other parties later on, to make up.'

'Not so many after that particular one. Soldiers' children are shunted off to boarding-school at an early age, to give them a settled environment for their education.'

'So are circus children, just the same,' Cara could not help exclaiming, and Tyler smiled.

'Another thing we have in common, *Cara mia*,' he murmured, too low for Beth to catch his words, and his smile widened into a grin at Cara's vitriolic look, and he raised his voice and said, 'About the balls . . .'

'I've seen a lot of big, brightly coloured balls in the department store in Broadwater,' Cara replied in a light, strictly business voice that drew a taunting look from Tyler, but she ignored it and went on, 'We'll be working there in a fortnight's time, so we might be able to purchase the balls for you at staff-discount rates.'

His eyes were still on her. Laughing at her. Knowing she could not rise to his *Cara mia* because her aunt was

with them. The tawny orbs were the colour of deep peat
pools, and tingles began inching up and down Cara's
spine, and to stop them she began to calculate
feverishly.

'Half a dozen big balls, and a dozen tennis balls,
should do. Then you could have a skittle-alley, like that
one over there.' In a desperate attempt to fend off his
look she pointed haphazardly in the general direction of
a well-patronised attraction nearby, and babbled on,
'That would be something a bit more challenging for
the older children. The same number of balls for each
booth would do.'

'We must have lots of balloons. Enough left over
in case some burst,' he said. The party again, Cara
thought, and quelled the reminder with a quick,

'The fair can provide those. They'll blow them up for
you as well.'

'And a candy-floss stall.'

'We've got candy-floss equipment at the circus, and a
stall to go with it.'

Courteously Tyler helped Beth Brook mount the
steps to the Wallaces' van, then as soon as she was
safely inside he took Cara by the elbow and said firmly,
'Before I decide on anything, I want to try out all these
things first myself to make sure they work.'

His eyes glinted down at her, challenging her to join
him, and Cara shrugged. 'You're the client,' she
answered indifferently. Her tone put him in his place,
and firmly established their business relationship.

Tyler grinned, completely unabashed by her manner,
and took her by the arm and steered her towards a
nearby candy-floss stall.

'Let's have a stick of candy-floss. It might get you in
the mood.'

'In the mood for what?' she asked tartly.

'Do you want me to answer that?' he grinned back,
and chuckled at her hasty, 'No!'

The candy-floss was pink and light and fluffy, and he
pulled a ball of it and held it to her mouth for her to
eat. As his fingers pushed the sweet concoction between
her teeth, they pressed down hard on her lower lip, a

deliberate, erotic pressure that curled her stomach into knots.

Her cheeks flamed, and she wondered wildly how she was going to cope with seeing him for the rest of the winter, when he could affect her like this in the middle of a crowded fairground.

His eyes watched the thoughts flit across her face, knew what they were, and laughed at them, and at things like business armour, and chaperoning crowds.

Cara spun away from him, turning her back. 'Let's have a look at the coconut-shy,' she said hurriedly.

Tyler followed close on her heels as she walked towards the booth; too close. The tingles began to spread along her spine, creeping underneath the armour. 'The last coconut I ate,' he remembered, 'I had to shin up a palm tree and cut it for myself.'

'Try for one with a ball. It'll be easier than climbing up a tree, and it'll keep your hands occupied at the same time,' she shot back acidly, and he laughed again.

'You throw as well.' He handed her three of his four balls.

'I know who I'd like to use as my target,' Cara muttered viciously, and threw one of the balls with a hopelessly bad aim.

'You'll have to do better than that at my Christmas party,' Tyler taunted, and told her without saying so that he wanted her to be there, as well as the coconut-shy.

As one of the attractions for his young guests, or for himself?

Cara glared, and threw the other two balls, and found to her disgust that her hands shook so much that her aim was even more erratic than before.

'It looks like I'll have to get the nut myself.'

He drew back his arm, and the clean line of him, and the latent power in his stance, made Cara draw in a swift breath. 'I hope you miss,' she hissed at him as he threw.

The nut toppled, hit amidships with clean accuracy. 'Unlikely,' he drawled with maddening complacency. 'No captain of the local cricket team would dare to miss such an easy throw.' He accepted the nut from the stall-holder, and cracked it expertly on the side of the booth. 'Have a piece,' he invited. 'And don't say, I don't want. It's hours until your next performance.'

Cara accepted the piece he gave her, rather than start an argument which she suspected she would lose anyway, and dug her teeth into the sweet white flesh, reflecting that a business relationship with Tyler was not proving any easier to control than a personal one.

They lost their money on the fruit machines, and tried their luck at the bowling-alley with little more success.

'Let's have a ride on the hobby-horses.' Tyler pulled Cara to a halt to watch as the big prancing mounts on the roundabout glided to a standstill.

'You're surely not thinking of having a roundabout at the party?' Cara protested.

'There's plenty of room outside in the Park if the weather stays mild,' he countered. 'Come on, let's get on.'

'You go by yourself.' Cara hung back. 'I—I don't much like the hobby-horses,' she admitted nervously.

'I don't believe it!' Tyler stared at her in undisguised amazement. 'You swing on the trapeze, balance on the high wire, and turn somersaults on Pride's back in the ring.'

So he had noticed her somersault. He could not know the reason for it, and Cara compressed her lips into silence. The reason was her secret, not to be shared with anyone, least of all with Tyler.

'Pride stays on the same level underneath me, even when she's galloping. The hobby-horses go up and down, as well as round and round, and they take my stomach with them,' she defended her cowardice.

'I'll hold you.'

Before she could protest, he circled her waist with his hands, and lifted her up on to the roundabout with him, and the crowd of people jostling to get on along with them made it impossible for her to put up any resistance.

What was worse, Cara discovered she did not want

to, as he drew her across his lap on the saddle of the nearest wooden horse, and held her tightly against him as the roundabout started off, and the horse began to go up and down, making escape impossible until it stopped.

Cara had once heard it said that it felt perfectly safe to walk across a quicksand until the very moment when the surface crust gave way, and it was too late to be able to scramble back to the safety of the bank.

She felt as if she were stepping on a quicksand now, and the crust was liable to give way at any minute. Nameless sensations flowed out from his grip on her, interfering with her breathing, and threatening to drag her under.

His voice in her ear said reassuringly, 'Hold on to me. You're quite safe.' And his mouth nuzzling her lobe turned the reassurance into a lie. Cara shivered. She was not safe anywhere near Tyler. And the danger lay as much in herself as in him.

'The ride's finished, or do you want to stay on for another go?'

The roundabout had stopped, and she had not noticed. Cara pulled herself upright on Tyler's lap, and her cheeks flushed a peony red as she met his laughing look, and her lashes dropped in confusion, shielding her eyes from the bright merriment in his.

'Not another. Let's go,' she said hurriedly.

Cara's flush deepened as she became conscious of amused looks from the people waiting to board the roundabout, and she struggled free from Tyler's arms and landed on the boards with a haste that made her stumble. She would have fallen if he had not been quick to grasp her, and he lifted her down and set her feet safely on the turf, and spared her feelings by suggesting lightly,

'There's the dodgem cars. Let's have a ride on those. They're steadier than the horses.'

They had to be steadier than her suddenly wobbly legs. Cara dropped thankfully into a car, and immediately regretted her capitulation as it moved off.

'This is great fun,' Tyler laughed. 'I haven't been on a

dodgem car for years.' He was like a boy released from school, and he enjoyed himself hugely.

The cars jostled and bumped and collided with one another, and desperate to remain anchored in her seat, Cara put her arms round as much of him as she could reach, and clung on to him like a limpet.

She now discovered that the boy she had glimpsed had been very fleetingly glimpsed only, and that the man was in firm control. He deliberately spun the car in dizzy circles in a highly successful attempt to make her cling to him even closer, experiencing sensations that had nothing to do with the dodgem car.

'You did that on purpose,' she accused him breathlessly when they regained terra firma. 'Just to make me hold on to you.' She was torn between fury and laughter at his outrageous behaviour.

Tyler grinned unrepentantly. 'You enjoyed it.'

It was useless to try to deny it, and he would not believe her if she did. But his words wiped away the laughter from Cara's face, and she felt suddenly cold. She must be totally transparent for Tyler to be able to read her so easily.

'All the fun of the fair,' a hoarse voice shouted, and the familiar, raucous cry was like a bitter warning.

That was all it was, to Tyler. Fun. A brief affair, with nothing further on his mind than to exploit a situation for his own ends, to while away the tedious winter months.

And for herself? The question sobered her.

There was no way she could avoid meeting Tyler, and she was dabbling with danger if she could not manage to bring under control the feelings that he was capable of producing in her, feelings that were only the automatic response of any normal woman to his extraordinary physical attraction.

Weren't they?

CHAPTER SIX

'LET's go back. We've looked at all the booths that are likedly to be of any use to you,' Cara urged. She felt the quicker she escaped back to the privacy of her van, the better.

'There's still the rifle range,' Tyler demurred.

'A rifle range is no use at a children's party.' Cara tried to walk past it, but Tyler's hand on her arm drew her back.

'There's no reason why we shouldn't have a go ourselves. It'll give me a bit of practice, and you need a vase to hold your rosebud,' he said casually, gesturing towards the variety of pottery-ware on offer as prizes.

Cara caught her breath. She had not expected him to allude to the rosebud so directly. 'How do you know I haven't already got a vase? We're circus people, not paupers,' she said proudly.

'I didn't suggest you were.' Tyler gave her an oblique look. 'But I can't imagine that life on the move is so very different for you, from the way it is for me when I'm on safari,' he said perceptively. 'Things that break or spill are luxuries that have to be done without, however pleasant they may make life in a more settled environment. The things we have in common seem to be mounting up,' he needled, his eyes watching Cara's heightened colour. 'Our lifestyles aren't all that different, when you come to think about it.'

She did not want to think about it. She watched under lowered lashes as he took the rifle handed to him by the booth-operator and squinted along the sights, and her heart did a quick somersault inside her breast.

So he must look when he is on safari, Cara thought. His eyes intent on the viewfinder of his camera. His whole attention concentrated on his subject, waiting for exactly the right moment to activate the shutter, that would come and be gone in split seconds, unrepeatable unless his reactions were lightning swift.

The incongruity of seeing the dedicated naturalist handling a death-dealing weapon suddenly struck her. He had criticised the circus way of life, and the opportunity to turn the tables on him was irresistible. She proceeded to turn them with relish.

'Surely you don't carry a rifle with you on safari?' she asked innocently. 'It seems hypocritical, to say the least, for a naturalist to go prepared to use a weapon.'

'Of course I carry a rifle with me when I'm in the field. Anyone who didn't would be a fool.' Tyler lowered the weapon and studied Cara with narrowed eyes. 'Not all of our subjects enjoy being photographed. Some of them make their feelings plain, sometimes violently. But we only ever shoot in self-defence, and then only as a very last resort,' he vindicated himself, and added unexpectedly, 'and for the pot, of course.'

That was an aspect of his travels that had not occurred to Cara. 'For the pot?' Her eyebrows arched her enquiry.

'On safari we have to travel even lighter than you do in your vans.' Tyler's lips gave a sudden tilt of amusement. 'One of your big living-vans would be regarded as the height of luxury by our team when we're in the field.'

No wonder he had appeared to be so at ease in Mitcham Brook's big van. Cara looked at him with new-seeing eyes as he continued casually,

'There aren't any shops in faraway places. Most of our storage space is given over to photographic equipment, and necessary medical supplies. Apart from basics like flour and sugar, we have to live mostly off the land.'

Noticing his easy handling of the weapon, Cara had no doubt the people in Tyler's team fared very well. Man, the eternal hunter. And not only of things to eat. She felt a quick sympathy with the paper target as his eyes dragged away, and he lifted the rifle once more to his shoulder, and aimed it at one of the small ringed squares hung in a row at the back of the booth.

'Four shots,' the booth-operator intoned.

Crack!

'You missed,' Cara jibed.

Tyler lifted careless shoulders. 'The sights need adjusting.'

'The poor worker always blames his tools.' Cara felt oddly disappointed. She had not expected him to be a poor loser.

'Each gun is different,' he answered indifferently. 'They need a bit of getting used to, that's all.' He fired again, into the black rings this time, and then again.

'You've clipped the edge of the bullseye.'

Sudden excitement sharpened Cara's attention, and her eyes riveted on the target. With caught breath she watched as Tyler lowered his head once more over the stock, and took aim for the last time.

Without quite knowing why, she suddenly wanted a vase from the booth. For the first time in her life she desired to possess something with a covetousness that frightened her, and all because Tyler had promised to win it for her. It was stupid and illogical, and she scorned herself because of it, but she stood beside him and willed him with all her power to win a vase for her.

Crack!

A tiny silence followed the last shot. It stretched into an aeon of uncertainty, and then the booth-operator spoke, and there was a wealth of respect in his voice.

'You're a good shot, guv'nor. Not many men get the measure of a strange rifle in only four shots.'

'Did you . . .?' Cara's throat felt oddly dry, and she swallowed, and tried again. 'I can't see another hole.'

'That's because the bullet's gone straight through the bullseye, miss. The hole looks as black as the ring.'

The booth-operator ripped off the paper target to show to her, and Cara took it from him with eager fingers, and held it up to the light, where the four holes showed clearly, marching in a confident line from the outside edge of the paper target to the exact centre.

'You've hit the bullseye.'

She tried to sound casual, but the shine in her eyes betrayed her.

'And you've won your vase.' He bent and lightly kissed the tip of her nose. 'Which one would you like?'

His action had the effect of scattering her senses into a confusion that made it totally impossible for her to decide. She hesitated for so long that Tyler became impatient.

'Have this one.' He picked up a slender white pottery specimen vase with a fluted rim, and the transfer of a pink rosebud on the one side. 'Take this as well, for a keepsake,' he added, and rolling the holed target into a thin spill he slid it part-way into the neck of the vase for safe carrying.

He pressed the two into her hands, and she said hurriedly, trying not to let her delight that he had won, show in her expression, 'I can see Aunt Beth just coming out of the Wallaces' van. It looks as if she might be having trouble getting away. I'd better go and rescue her. Mrs Wallace is unstoppable once she starts to talk.'

It was she who needed rescuing, not the other way round, Cara reflected as she hurried across the grass, acutely conscious of Tyler's lithe, silent stride beside her, of the vase, a slender hardness in her hands.

'You can finish your talk tomorrow,' Cara promised the still voluble Mrs Wallace when they reached the van. 'Otherwise, Aunt Beth won't be back in time to help Uncle Mitch get ready for the evening performance.'

Unconsciously she sighed. Always, it was the next performance. Suddenly the circus seemed like some terrible taskmaster, demanding every moment of their lives. She looked up and became conscious that Tyler's eyes were on her, and guiltily she switched off her thoughts, as if the tawny orbs could read right into them.

'We haven't got halfway through our talk yet,' Mrs Wallace chuckled good-humouredly, and her bright eyes darted over Tyler with undisguised interest.

'Come *on*, you'll be late.' Cara caught the look, and redoubled her efforts to extricate her aunt. Mrs Wallace's tongue was known to be as tactless as it was long, and her curiosity was insatiable.

'Beth still hasn't got round to telling me when you

and Gio are getting married,' the fairground woman
steamrollered on.

'We're not,' Cara retorted, with such force that Mrs
Wallace's eyebrows shot up.

'Well, I never,' she exclaimed. 'Gio seemed to take it
for granted . . .'

'And apparently made sure everyone else did the
same,' Cara returned with asperity.

'Still being your own person, *Cara mia*?' Tyler
enquired softly, and Cara ground her teeth in frustrated
silence as she finally managed to part the two friends,
and steer her aunt on a course towards their own camp.

'Have you seen any booths that would be suitable for
your party?' Beth Brook chatted amiably as they
walked.

'I've decided upon three.' Tyler did not say which
they were, and determinedly Cara clamped her lips
together, refusing to allow her curiosity to show.

'Is that a vase you've got?' Beth turned bright eyes on
the fluted porcelain in Cara's hands. 'It's pretty.'

'Tyler won it at the rifle range. I'll show it to you
later. Time's getting on, and I've got Pride and the
ponies to see to.'

Swiftly Cara marshalled excuses in her mind to
prevent Tyler from coming with her to the ponies, and
felt curiously flat when he did not offer to, and
commented instead,

'I'll see you tomorrow to discuss details of the party
booking. About what time?'

'Tomorrow's Sunday, and we always hold a service in
the big top after the morning chores are done. It's
usually over by about half past ten. I'll ride across to
the Hall when it's finished.'

Which relegated Tyler and his children's party to
second place in her list of priorities, and had the
advantage of pushing the appointment as late into the
morning as possible, so that she need not spend any
more time in his company than she was absolutely
obliged to. Which gave Cara a feeling of immense
satisfaction on both counts.

'See you then,' Tyler nodded, and leaving Cara at the

steps to her van he stood chatting for a moment to Beth before he strolled away towards where his Jaguar was parked beside her uncle's Rover.

Linda's voice arrested Cara as she was about to enter her van, and she turned reluctantly, conscious of the other girl's eyes flitting over her, noticing the vase, even the target tucked into the top. Missing nothing, and putting two and two together and making six, Cara guessed vexedly.

'Giving you presents now, is he?' Linda sneered. 'I wonder what Gio will think of that?'

'It's none of Gio's business. In any case, it's hardly a present. He won it at the rifle range, and I can't imagine Lord Broadwater would want a vase of this sort for himself.'

Honesty often had the effect of disarming people, Cara thought hopefully, but Linda had other arrows in her quiver, and seeing that she had missed the first time, she shot again.

'It's no use you getting any fancy notions about Lord-high-and-mighty Broadwater,' she said maliciously. 'Someone else got there first.' There was a folded piece of paper in Linda's hand, and she thrust it at Cara. 'Take a good look at the competition, and ask yourself if you're in the same league,' she said spitefully, and before Cara could reply she flounced away back towards the tent.

It was the front cover of *Personalities*, an exclusive quarterly magazine dated early that year, Cara saw. She shut her van door behind her, and put the vase down on the table, and spread out the page beside it.

The eye-catching caption read, 'This year's most eligible bachelor. Fascinating details of his life story inside.'

The photograph was a full-length one, taken at some official function or other. No doubt the article inside the magazine would tell the reader just what.

Tyler was in evening dress. He looked almost unbelievably handsome. The stark black and white suited him, making him look even taller, if possible, showing off to advantage his tanned features, and the rich colour of his hair. His head was slightly bent, inclined towards the upturned face of the girl who hung on his arm, and they were laughing into one another's eyes.

The girl, Cara saw with an inexplicable pang, was quite stunningly beautiful. Blinking, she thought, 'It's a good job I'm not in competition, like Linda imagines. It would take Miss World to compete successfully with that.'

The girl was taller than Cara herself. Her head reached slightly past Tyler's shoulder. Just the right height to lean on it. The thought strayed through Cara's mind, and she pushed it out again, and concentrated on the rest of the details of the girl's appearance.

Her hair was gold, with a slight hint of auburn in it, and cut in short soft curls framing a delicately boned face. Cara could not see the colour of her eyes, but guessed green from the clear jade of the girl's dress.

'Which is about the shade mine must look now,' she thought, sucking in her breath. The long, flowing lines of the girl's dress hugged its wearer's slender figure as if she had been poured into it, and every minute detail screamed 'Paris model'. An orchid, only slightly paler than the dress, graced one creamy shoulder.

Cara turned the page over, and was dismayed to find that her fingers were unsteady, but the article must have started further inside the magazine, because the reverse of the cover contained nothing more illuminating than an advertisement for a well-known brand of shampoo.

Afterwards, the ponies seemed to take an age to deal with on her own, made no easier by Gio interrupting her work before Cara was half-way through. Her partner was spoiling for a fight, Cara saw warily, watching him approach, and decided upon attack rather than defence.

'Don't *you* start asking me about that rose,' she thrust before Gio could speak. 'I'm sick to death of hearing about it. If I'd known the trouble it would cause, I'd have thrown it right back again. That is, if I knew who to throw it at. I'm not responsible if a hyped-up member of the audience starts tossing flowers into the ring.'

'I didn't say you were.' Gio looked taken aback by her attack. 'But you must know that it would be Broadwater who threw it.'

'How should I know? There was no message with it,' Cara said sharply. 'And now for goodness' sake let's talk about something else. You haven't heard the latest about the children's party at the Hall.'

Cunningly she deprived Gio of the opportunity of bringing up the matter himself, and gave him, unasked, a brief edited rundown of her tour of the fair with Tyler. How brief, and how edited, she hoped fervently Gio would not guess.

'Uncle Mitch suggested the idea,' she finished offhandedly, 'and it seemed to take on. It will bring the Wallaces some useful extra business, as well as us, although Ty ... Lord Broadwater didn't say which booths he wanted, when he left Aunt Beth and me just now.'

Cara held her breath, but Gio did not appear to have noticed her slip, and her reference to Beth Brook being with them further defused her partner's temper to the point when he merely remarked sarcastically,

'Perhaps Broadwater wants to discuss it with his girlfriend first.'

Cara lifted one shoulder, and said lightly, 'You mean the girl on the cover of that magazine? Linda showed it to me, though I can't imagine why. Lord Broadwater's private life is nothing to do with us.'

Once again her strategy worked, and to Cara's relief the evening performance passed uneventfully, although for herself it fell flat after the previous one, and the sparkle was gone again. And when, the next morning, the gathering in the big top broke up, she slipped away unnoticed while Gio was talking to some of the people from the fairground who had joined them for the Sunday service. The last thing she wanted was for her partner to accompany her, as he would insist upon doing if he knew where she was going.

Mrs Wallace and Beth were headed towards the

latter's van in search of a cup of coffee. Cara refused their invitation to join them, and hurried into a change of clothes, a refuge from both Gio and her aunt's voluble visitor.

And from the haunting fragrance of the rosebud, that stood in its brand-new vase on her dressing-table, and conjured up visions of Tyler, and the girl in the Paris model dress hanging on his arm, each time the bloom caught her eye.

She tucked a notebook, ball-point pen, and measuring-tape into the pocket of her slacks, and reflected ruefully that they were not much use as business armour, but since they were all she had, they would have to do. In that mood, she harnessed Pride and was away from the circus camp before the rest of the troupe began to emerge from the big top.

At the Hall she left the mare in the care of the groom, and braced herself as she mounted the entrance steps, and gave the old-fashioned bell-pull a tug that sent the echoes ringing through the house.

A deep-throated barking answered the noise, and Daniels appeared, smiling a greeting as Cara announced, 'I've come about the arrangements for the children's party at Christmas.'

Tyler was expecting her, so why did he not come to the door to meet her himself? she wondered disgruntled. Although she was reluctant to admit it, she had kept a watchful eye open for him while she rode across the Park, wondering if he might ride to meet her, and felt curiously deflated when he did not put in an appearance, and she had to make the journey on her own.

Perhaps it was Tyler's way of putting her in her place, and making sure she did not get ideas above her station, she told herself caustically. Linda's remark about her not being in the same league still rankled.

'Yes, I know,' Daniels answered her genially. 'Tyler's expecting you. I'll take you straight through to the ballroom now, and he'll join you in a few minutes. He's engaged at the moment.'

The classic excuse, Cara thought cynically, and tilted

her nose in the air to show that it was a matter of total indifference to her whether Tyler was here to greet her or not.

In doing so, she caught a faint waft of perfume that set her pulses racing as she walked beside Daniels through the entrance hall.

Roses?

Surely the fragrance could not have followed her here from her van? Capturing her mind to such an extent that she could actually smell it? Cara looked round her, startled, and her eyes lit on a silver rose bowl full of blooms, set on a low polished table in a corner, gently spilling their perfume into the surrounding air like an omen. Tyler's voice spoke,

'Thank you for coming to tell me, Luke. I've had half a dozen phone calls in the last half-hour, telling me they'd strayed. Have they all been rounded up now?'

The deep sound of a country voice answered, 'Aye, gaffer,' and then Tyler's voice resumed,

'Good. Fix a padlock to the gate as soon as possible, will you? There should be one in the estate stores. The cowman can carry a key, and when people find the gate locked, it'll force them to use the stile instead of taking the easy way through the gate on to the footpath.'

Tyler's voice came firm and strong through the half-open library door, and unconsciously Cara's feet slowed to a halt beside it.

'This way, Miss Varelli.'

She came to herself with a start to see Daniels holding open a door into a room which she had never seen before. She hurried to catch up with him, vexed that he might suspect her of eavesdropping.

'Perhaps you'd like to look at the room while you're waiting? I've pushed the dividing screen right back to give you an idea of how it will be for the children's party.'

How it was, was immense. From previous visits to the Hall, Cara was already familiar with the library and the drawing-room, but the sheer size of the ballroom made her blink. It also made her feel very small and insignificant. Perhaps Tyler intended that, too?

'Sorry to keep you waiting. Some idiot left a field gate open, and the cattle strayed half through the village. The estate foreman just came in to let me know they were all rounded up again.'

Tyler was beside her before Cara was aware of his approach. Soft-soled shoes in chocolate-brown suede, to match his slim-fitting corduroy casuals, explained his silent approach, and a gold-and-brown spotted cravat knotted loosely at the neck of his cream silk shirt complemented his own vivid colouring with an effect that made her knees feel strangely weak.

He regarded her for a moment lazily, and then his eyes slid round the room. 'What, no Gio?' he exclaimed in exaggerated surprise. 'Didn't he want to come along with you, to make sure you didn't meet a fate worse than death?'

'Gio wasn't asked,' Cara retorted sharply. 'And I'm perfectly capable of taking care of myself, without Gio tagging along.' That was not true, at least so far as Tyler was concerned, but it made her feel better to say it. 'I don't take along members of the troupe when I go out on business engagements for Uncle Mitch. For that matter, I don't usually deal with them on a Sunday anyway, it's our only day off during the week,' she finished carelessly.

The 'business engagements' helped her knees considerably, she found, and she faced Tyler with returning confidence until he drawled,

'But you came here this morning, Cara, didn't you?'

The inference was obvious, and it stung her into a swift retort. 'Not for you,' she disabused him. 'I came because Uncle Mitch wanted me to.'

'Ah yes, Mitch. A very knowledgeable man, your uncle.' From Tyler's deadpan expression, Cara could not be sure whether he was needling her or not, and she decided not to risk finding out.

'He wants to gain a bit more knowledge from you.' Carefully she steered the conversation back on to lines she felt she could handle. 'He wants to know how many children will be coming to the party, for a start. We don't want to bring along masses too much candy-floss, and twice the number of balloons you need.'

She pulled out her notebook and ball-point pen from her slacks pocket, and tried not to see the satirical lift to Tyler's lips as he murmured, 'All very efficient, I see,' and answered her question with a thoughtful, 'Mmm. Let me see. At Daniels' last count, there were sixty-five children altogether, but there may be some more. Better cater for eighty, just in case.'

In spite of herself, Cara's eyes rounded. 'That sounds like the entire contents of the village school,' she exclaimed.

The party was supposed to be for the estate workers' children, and her mind boggled. Either the estate workers were extraordinarily prolific, or the estate was a good deal larger than she had previously realised.

'It's all the pupils from the local school, plus their teachers, and the extra numbers will take in the children from the circus as well. Ask your aunt to invite them for me, will you?'

'Don't tell me you've accepted our circus to that extent?' Cara jibed with mocking incredulity.

'I don't discriminate against children. Nor against all grown-ups, for that matter,' Tyler retorted significantly, and left the sentence in mid-air, waiting for Cara to ask which grown-ups he excluded.

'Tell me which booths you want from the fair.'

She ducked his question, and asked one of her own, and Tyler's eyes glinted, knowing that she was merely putting off the time when she must ask him which acts he wanted from the big top.

Cara's stomach churned, wondering what his answer would be. She wrote down the booths he dictated. Coconut-shy. Skittle-alley. Hoopla stall. All the time warily conscious of him looking over her shoulder as he dictated his wants.

Her nape pricked at his closeness, and she felt the faint fan of his breath a persuasive pleasure against her cheek. Her pulses pounded in response like aspen leaves trembling to a breeze, and made it difficult for her to focus on the page, and more difficult still to write legibly.

Shakily, Cara wished he would go and stand somewhere else. While Tyler stood over her, her mind refused to concentrate on what she was doing. Only her senses seemed alive, clamouring with an insistence that deafened her to all else except his tall length, bending slightly so that he could read across her shoulder what she was writing down.

'That deals with the fairground booths. Now to the acts from the big top,' Tyler said, broaching the subject himself, and Cara tensed. The tantalising undertone of his voice told her he was deliberately keeping her in suspense.

He wanted the clown, and the magician, and the girl who juggled the balls with her feet, and he watched closely as Cara wrote down, 'Ben, Pepi, and Linda,' and then waited, with her pencil poised.

Surely those would be enough, with the three booths from the fair? There would not be sufficient time left to fit in a Father Christmas if he had any more. Suddenly she had to know. Her stomach tightened until she began to feel physically sick, and it sent an urgent message to her tongue, which blurted of its own accord, 'Any more? Anything that needs the big apparatus?'

'No.' Tyler shook his head adamantly. Cara's fingers tightened convulsively about the ball-point pen, and only by a supreme effort did she manage to school her features into a mask to hide the lurch of irrational disappointment that made her heart a sudden pain in her breast. She could feel Tyler's eyes on her, watching for her reaction, and when she remained silent he said,

'It wouldn't be wise to have the apparatus acts. It's one thing for the children to watch them at the circus, but if they see the same thing in a private house, they might be tempted to try it out for themselves when they get home, and I don't want broken bones to follow their party.'

'A private house!' Cara ejaculated, her eyes swivelling round the enormous room, and laughter that had a tinge of hysteria in it bubbled up inside her, threatening her self-control.

'The Hall is larger than the cottages the children come from, but it's still a private house—a home. It's not a circus ring.'

Patently it was not, and the difference acted like a cold douche, sobering Cara. Not in the same league, she thought murderously, and ground out aloud, 'That's the lot, then.'

Her ball-point pen scored a savage line below her notes. So great was the pressure she put on it that the pen-point dug into the lined paper, and made a deep rent across the page. Over her bent head, Cara felt Tyler's glance rake the page of her notebook, noting the jagged tear.

'Not quite.' His hands came up, and took her by the shoulders, and turned her round to face him.

Cara could feel the pressure of each separate finger and thumb scorch through the chunky wool of her sweater, and she took in a shuddering breath as one hand left her shoulder and caught her by the chin, and tipped up her face to meet his own.

Her lashes flew back, and she stared wide-eyed into his face, and he said, 'There *is* one more I want, Cara. You.'

He lowered his head, and his lips brushed lightly across her mouth. Her notebook slipped from her hand and thudded softly on to the floor, followed by the ball-point pen, loosed by her suddenly nerveless fingers, but Cara heard neither of them fall.

She could hear only the pounding of the blood in her ears, and Tyler's voice saying, 'You.' And then his lips were on her cheeks, her eyes, her hair . . .

'You're lovely, *Cara mia*,' he murmured, and the rumble of his voice was like the deep purring of a big cat inside his chest.

Never touch a tiger.

Or allow the tiger to touch her?

His touch was electric. Demoralising. It roused passions that she could not control. Frightening passions, that made her want to beg him to hold her even closer, and at the same time made her want to run away. Her eyes were wild as she strained away from him, pushing at him with hands that felt as weak as her shaking knees.

'Don't call me that.'

'Still fighting, Cara? Still playing wildcat?'

'I didn't come here to p-play,' she stammered. 'I came to talk business. To talk about the party.'

'Is that *all* you came for, *Cara mia*? Sure?'

'Of course I'm sure. What else?'

'For this?' he suggested softly, and kissed her again.

His lips sent fire racing through her veins, burning her up, threatening to consume her. She made a last desperate bid to retreat to the safety of her business armour.

'You said you w-wanted me to . . .'

'Don't *you* want *me*, Cara?' The ball of his thumb stroked the nape of her neck with a light, sensuous movement that sent tremors running the length of her spine.

'No!' she exploded. She wrenched herself violently free from his hold. 'No. I—you—you're a client. Nothing more.'

She faced him, at bay, her eyes huge and black and glittering in a face that had gone chalk-white.

'Being a client is as good a base as any to start from.' Tyler eyed her narrowly, and Cara dropped her lashes, shielding her eyes lest he should read in them—what? Bewilderedly, she was at a loss to name her feelings herself.

'You've dropped your notebook and pencil.' Tyler picked them up and glanced down at her list. 'You haven't added your own lasso-dancing act,' he said, and handed them back to her. 'Better do it now, in case you forget.'

As if she was likely to forget. She snatched book and pencil from his hand and began feverishly to write, not caring that the script that resulted was an illegible scrawl.

'I thought the lasso-dancing was extremely clever. Fascinating to watch,' Tyler said urbanely. 'It's something the children could try for themselves with perfect safety afterwards.'

Her own safety was more at risk than that of the children, Cara decided raggedly, and took a deep, steadying breath before venturing, 'Uncle Mitch sent you a list of measurements of all the booths you'd be likely to be interested in. He got them from Mr Wallace, in case you wanted to measure up the room.'

Cara pulled the slip of paper out of her pocket, and the tape measure came out along with it.

Tyler's hand reached for the list, but she backed away warily, and put it down instead on a nearby table-top for him to pick up for himself, and pretended to be engrossed in rolling up the measuring-tape.

His eyes laughed at her retreat, and her colour rose, but resolutely she carried on rolling.

Surreptitiously Cara watched him pick up the paper and study it, and his eyes measured her when he looked up and said, 'I'll measure, if you'll hold the other end of the tape for me.'

Cara hesitated for only a moment. The tape was six feet long, and he would be at a nice safe distance if he held one end, while she held the other. 'Suits me,' she said briefly, and flipped the rolled-up tape loose again towards him.

He caught it with dextrous fingers, and his grin mocked her, but all he said was, 'I thought of putting the hoopla stall about here. The coconut-shy and the skittle-alley could go one on each side of it. I'll put a light chalk line on the floor to mark the frontage of each booth. Bring the tape to this side, first. We'll start to measure from here.'

Tyler walked over to the place he indicated, and Cara followed him, still holding on to her end of the tape.

Like a puppy-dog on the end of a lead, she thought, nettled, but if she dropped her end she would have to go close to Tyler again to pick it up, so with an ill grace she held on to it and followed him.

'That's about right. Hold your end there.' Tyler hunkered down and put his end of the tape on the floor, and Cara followed suit, her breathing returning to normal now he was at a safer distance.

'Pull the tape tight, so that I can run the chalk along

it in a straight line,' he commanded, and proceeded to halve the distance between them.

Cara watched him approach her with growing apprehension, chalking carefully as he came along the edge of the tightly held tape.

A pulse began a slow thudding in her throat, and panic started to build up inside her as he got steadily closer. She wanted to loose her end of the tape, but if she did he would know she was afraid. And why.

Slowly the chalk line advanced, bringing Tyler with it another couple of feet closer to her. In desperation, Cara knelt and made a long arm, holding the end of the tape with the very tip of her finger.

The pulse became rampant, suffocating her. He was barely a foot away now. He looked up and grinned into her wide eyes. His face was on a level with her own, and she stared mesmerised as it reached out towards her.

'Lunch is served, my lord.'

Cara sat back on her heels and felt slightly dizzy. The young maid she had seen before tapped across the room towards them on proudly new court shoes.

'Thank you, Jill. Tell Mrs Turner we'll be ready in about five minutes, will you?'

Tyler thanked the maid with a smile, and unhurriedly finished his chalk-mark on the floor, right to the very tip of Cara's finger. She withdrew it as if the chalk were hot, and demanded unsteadily, 'What do you mean, *we'll* be ready?'

'You and me,' Tyler retorted imperturbably. 'It'd be churlish of me to refuse you lunch after you've taken the trouble to come all this way to—er—work, on your Sunday off.' His eyes mocked her indecision.

Cara compressed her lips. Her hardest task had been to cope with Tyler—or herself?—and the decision was no trouble at all. She refused his invitation almost with a sense of anti-climax.

'Thanks, but I can't stay. Aunt Beth's expecting me back for lunch.'

'On the contrary, I mentioned to her yesterday when we parted company, that I'd be expecting you to stay and have lunch with me today,' Tyler contradicted. 'She won't be expecting you back, so there'll be no lunch prepared for you if you go. And since you haven't got a show this afternoon, there's nothing to stop you from eating in the middle of the day,' he demolished her only remaining excuse.

'I'm not dressed to have lunch out,' Cara protested lamely.

Aunt Beth had not mentioned anything about her having lunch at the Hall. Probably she thought Tyler had already invited her, and she had accepted.

'You look fine to me.' His gaze raked over her, warming her cheeks. 'But the food won't be, if we keep it waiting, and I refuse to offend my housekeeper. Mrs Turner's a superb cook.'

The lunch was simple, but supremely good, and justified Tyler's praise of his housekeeper.

A rich, creamy soup was followed by roast pheasant, with tiny button sprouts whose delicious freshness had to be home-grown, along with glazed carrots and game chips flanked by stuffed bacon rolls, and followed by a raspberry soufflé so light that it rivalled the candy-floss they had eaten at the fair.

The repast was served in a small ante-room off the vast dining-room. A small table had been set for two, and pushed into a deep bay window overlooking the garden and the Park.

Early jasmine made a bright splash of colour from a crystal vase set on a low window-sill, and the morning's papers, and one or two current periodicals, lay on an occasional table beside an easy chair drawn close to the log fire.

This homely evidence of occupation told Cara that this was the room where Tyler spent his brief leisure hours, when he was freed from his writing, and the duties of the estate.

A well-filled bookcase stood beside the easy chair, packed, Cara noted alertly, with volumes in modern bindings. Most probably Tyler's own books, she surmised, and not some he had inherited. She felt a sudden curiosity to see what the titles were, and through them gain some further insight into the character of their owner.

In spite of its comfortable, lived-in look, the room was filled with priceless pieces, she saw. Her own interest in antiques, which because of lack of space she could only indulge by reading instead of actual collecting, told her that the chair she sat on was Chippendale, and the Ming vase that stood on an inlaid rosewood table in a corner of the room would be enough by itself to buy out the circus a dozen times over.

Far from looking ostentatious, the priceless artifacts fitted into their ancient background as if they had grown there.

Not so herself, Cara thought uncomfortably. In her workmanlike outfit of sweater and slacks, neat enough for the job she had come to do, but well worn and several times washed, she felt as out of place as if a modern chromium monstrosity had been introduced among the hand-carved furniture.

It spoiled her appetite for her excellent lunch, and sensitively she imagined the maid's eyes on her as she served, probably criticising her clothes.

Tyler's own casual outfit looked just right. He blended into his surroundings like one of the original paintings hanging on the walls.

Just so would the girl on the magazine cover blend in with this background, Cara thought with a tightening of her throat that made it unexpectedly difficult to swallow the last few spoonfuls of the super-light soufflé.

The girl who hung on Tyler's arm in the photograph would fit into these surroundings with the same easy grace as Tyler himself.

They were both in the same league.

CHAPTER SEVEN

THE week dragged. Persistent rain streamed from leaden skies, and denied Cara and the mare their usual morning exercise.

Wednesday saw the last performance in the big top for that winter, and afterwards there was only the daily stint of chores with the animals, and practice in the ring to keep Cara occupied until the first of the private bookings in the local store on Saturday.

Tyler came to the circus twice during the week, but on each occasion Mitcham Brook accompanied him to look at the ponies, and Tyler had no opportunity to speak to Cara alone.

She was glad, she told herself fiercely, and wondered at the strange restlessness that pursued her, refusing to allow her to settle to any of her long-looked-forward-to hobbies, now that she had some spare time on her hands.

A faint glimmer of sunshine breaking through the grey on the Saturday morning brought some relief from the gloom that had settled over her, and she told her aunt at breakfast,

'I'll go into Broadwater early, and do some Christmas shopping before we give the performance in the store this afternoon.'

Anything, Cara thought, would be better than dragging out another empty morning at the circus.

'I'll come with you,' Gio said promptly, overhearing her remark as he dropped in at the van to return a tool he had borrowed from Mitch.

'You know you can't. You've got to transport our apparatus in the van, and erect it in the store ready for the performance this afternoon.' Cara instantly blocked his suggestion.

Desperately she felt she needed to be alone for a while. To lose herself in the anonymity of the Christmas

shopping crowds, and for a short time at least, forget
the circus, and Gio. And Tyler, if that were possible.

His clean-cut features, and the sound of his deep,
resonant voice, occupied her thoughts too often for her
peace of mind, and the uncanny effect he had on her
whenever she was anywhere near him was even more
disturbing.

Her wish to lose herself in the crowds was amply
fulfilled when she reached the store. It was packed with
Saturday shoppers, and her small frame was hustled
and buffeted as she battled her way round the counters.

But the bright scarlet track-suit which she wore in
obedience to her terms of contract with the store singled
her out for special attention from the assistants, and she
speedily acquired the items she had come to buy. She
hesitated between an Arran sweater and a gold ball-
point pen for her uncle.

In the end she decided upon both. The pen was a
particularly nice one, in a neat presentation case, and it
would do for her uncle's birthday which came late in
January. Cara wrinkled her nose at the smell from the
bottle of Gio's favourite hair-oil, and thrust it to the
bottom of her bag before she made her way to the
sports department to join her partner for the
performance.

'You've cut it fine,' Gio grumbled when she
appeared. 'I thought you were never coming. What kept
you until now?'

'I was finishing my Christmas shopping. You can see
how packed the store is.'

'Hurry up and change,' Gio urged. 'I'll hold your bag
for you.'

'There's no need. I've come ready dressed in my
costume under the track-suit,'

Swiftly Cara unzipped the suit and rolled it into a
ball on the top of her shopping, and gave the bag into
the care of a smiling store assistant as the manager's
voice rallied the watching shoppers.

'Ladies and gentlemen. Cara and Gio, from Mitcham
Brook's famous circus, have consented to . . .'

The familiar build-up to the familiar routine, in

essence no different because it was for a sales promotion in a store instead of a performance in the big top. The store's central heating was almost overpowering, much worse than the big top, thought Cara in perspiring discomfort as she mounted the steps on to the platform with Gio.

The cool draught was welcome, and brought her some relief as she swung on the trapeze with Gio. And then she went icy cold as she looked down and saw Tyler's tawny crown in among the shopping crowd below her. He stood out a head's height above the rest of the people, and as he looked up to watch her perform his stare trapped and held her.

One, two, buckle my shoe. Three, four, shut the door. Cara counted fiercely, shutting the door of her mind on Tyler, and forcing herself to concentrate on her routine.

His hair shone like a sun below her, pulling her eyes, but mercifully the performance was only a short one. Even for a sales promotion the store did not want to distract its customers for too long from the serious business of making purchases, and Cara felt a wave of relief as the routine came to an end.

She ran back to floor level and zipped herself back into her track-suit, then dutifully did a series of handstands round the roped-off enclosure. The combination of track-suit, central heating, and exercise brought her temperature back to melting point, and she felt as if her cheeks must match the colour of the suit when she finally straightened up, and bowed smiling to acknowledge the burst of clapping that broke from the assembled shoppers.

'As you can see, ladies and gentlemen, Cara and Gio both wear our brand-name track-suits, the perfect garments for the discerning sports enthusiast, and an ideal Christmas gift . . .'

The manager intoned his commercial, the performance was over, and the crowd began slowly to move away. Gio said, 'Go and wait for me in the van. I'll dismantle the apparatus, and join you there in about half an hour or so.'

'I'll have another look round the store until you're

ready,' Cara retorted. She did not particularly want to brave the crowd in the store again, and a breath of fresh air would have been welcome, but she rebelled at Gio's peremptory tone. Also, she urgently wanted to lose herself in the crowds in case Tyler should take it into his head to come across to the enclosure to speak to herself and Gio. She felt she could not cope with the two of them together. 'I'll go and have another look round while we're here, and *you* can wait for *me* in the van,' she told her partner mutinously, and turned to duck under the ropes.

'As you're free, it seems an appropriate time to enlist your help,' Tyler's voice butted in smoothly, and he stepped easily over the ropes of the enclosure to join them.

She was too late. Cara stood still, dismayed. Gio straightened up from what he was doing and eyed the other man belligerently. 'Cara's already done her shopping,' he scowled.

'This isn't shopping. It's business,' Tyler replied, completely unruffled by Gio's undisguised hostility.

Cara watched the two men apprehensively. 'For goodness' sake, don't make a scene in the store,' she begged Gio, and turned to Tyler. 'Uncle Mitch takes all the new bookings.' Urgently she tried to smooth over the mounting anger that flushed her partner's face. His temper under stress was always unpredictable, and it would do nothing for the image of the circus if he had a tantrum in public.

'It isn't a new booking. It's about the balls for the coconut-shy at the party. You promised to obtain them for me from the store,' Tyler reminded her, and added equably, 'Now would be an ideal opportunity, while we're both here, and free.'

'I'll have a word with the manager for you,' Cara hedged. 'He'll take you to the toy department to choose what you want for yourself.'

'I think it's better for a lady to choose things for children, don't you?' Tyler returned pleasantly, and cupped his hand under Cara's elbow. 'Have you got everything? Let's go.'

'Cara isn't free. She's staying here, with me,' Gio snarled, and stepped forward, his fists beginning to ball.

The sight of his clenched hands was all that was needed to make up Cara's mind. 'I'm not hanging about here for half an hour while you dismantle the apparatus,' she flung over her shoulder, and slipping between the two men she was out of the enclosure, and melting into the crowd, before either of them had time to grasp her intention.

She hurried away from the sports department, in what direction she neither knew nor cared, so long as it was away from Tyler and Gio, but before she had gone many yards a hand came to rest lightly on her shoulder, steering her.

At first she responded to it blindly, and then awareness came, and the now familiar leaping of her pulses told her who the hand belonged to, and she turned on Tyler and demanded angrily, 'Did you *have* to provoke Gio? Surely you could have chosen a few coloured balls for yourself?'

'I don't imagine it takes much to provoke Gio,' Tyler responded, and there was steel underlying his tone. 'Does he respond with his fists when *you* provoke him?' he enquired with silky smoothness.

'Of course not,' Cara flashed indignantly.

'I should hope not.' The steel was still there, and then it was hidden as Tyler urged her forward to choose from among the piles of big, brightly coloured kicking-balls, and soft, creamy tennis balls, and took out his cheque book to settle for them while the assistant dropped them into a large net for ease of carrying.

'Drat this pen!' Tyler scowled as the instrument refused to write.

'Does it need a refill? We sell them at the counter over there.' The assistant pointed helpfully.

'No, unfortunately it needs a new barrel. This one got damaged a few months ago, and it hasn't worked properly since. It seems to have packed up altogether now,' Tyler answered resignedly.

'Have mine.' Cara delved into her handbag and

brought out the one she always carried with her for emergencies.

Tyler took it and made out his cheque, and when he had finished with it he absentmindedly tucked it into the top pocket of his jacket. Cara made no comment. It was only a throwaway plastic pen, and she had several more still unused in the packet in her van. She forgot about it as Tyler slung the net of balls across his shoulder and commented amusedly, 'If I fall over while I'm carrying these, I'll bounce.'

The germ of an idea tugged at the back of Cara's mind, but before it could take shape Tyler said, 'Let's have a cup of coffee before we make our way back to the car park.' He gave an observant glance at her flushed face. 'You look as if you could do with a drink.'

'I'm cooked inside this beastly track-suit,' Cara admitted.

'Unzip it.'

'I daren't. I've only got my ring costume on underneath.'

'I shan't object,' he grinned.

Cara made a face at him. 'I object, strongly,' she retorted, and left the track-suit firmly zipped up to her chin. 'Scanty costume is fine in the big top, but not in public outside.'

'It'll be cooler in the coffee bar.' Tyler steered her through the glass doors, under whirring fans that brought a welcome breath of air to her hot cheeks.

'Let's sit at the bar,' Cara said. Away from the crush of the crowds she felt vulnerable, and headed for the more populated bar-stools.

'It's quieter here, at a table.' Tyler took their tray of coffee and turned her instead towards a table placed in a deserted corner. 'The bar-stools are too tall for you anyway. They're built for lanky individuals, like me.'

Lanky was not the word Cara would have used to describe him. Superbly tall would be more fitting. She sat down on the chair he held out for her, and kept her eyes lowered, trying not to look at him as she concentrated on stirring her coffee.

'When do you want the fairground booths delivered

to the Hall, ready for the party?' she blurted at last, when the coffee was stirred to distraction, and the silence was fast reaching a dead end which Tyler did not seem inclined to break.

'Tuesday morning will do. The party doesn't start until half past three.' Tyler roused out of his reverie, and asked, 'What about returning the booths? Will the fairground people want them back the same evening?'

'No. The booths they send to you will be spares. They always keep one or two extra, in case of emergencies, or for hire.'

Business talk. Impersonal talk. A nice, safe topic of conversation that got Cara through her cup of coffee, and when it was finished, and she began to falter, a vigilant waitress saved her by hurrying across and whipping away her empty cup.

'Have you finished with your cup, love? And you, sir? I'll take them with me. I might as well give the table a wipe while I'm here.'

The girl flapped her cloth briskly across the table top, and Cara jumped thankfully to her feet. 'We'd better go. Gio will be waiting for me in the van.'

'We mustn't keep Gio waiting, whatever happens.'

Cara ignored the thin edge of sarcasm that sharpened Tyler's voice, and headed out of the coffee bar in nervous haste, that she hoped he would attribute to her anxiety not to keep her partner waiting.

She was uneasily conscious of him close behind her as they threaded their way towards the exit, and she drew a deep draught of cool air when at last they emerged on to the car park.

It steadied her feet to a more normal pace, although her pulse-rate refused to follow suit, especially when Tyler cupped his hand round her elbow as they crossed the tarmac to where the circus van was parked.

'I've been waiting here for you, for ages,' Gio snapped ill-temperedly as they approached, and Tyler answered suavely,

'In that case, you can get going right away.' His level look held that of the trapeze man, and it was Gio's eyes that shifted away first.

He flung into the cab of the van, and slammed the door to behind him, and Cara walked moodily round the back to reach the passenger side. It would be a dreadful journey back to the circus. She raised her hand to open the van door, but Tyler forestalled her.

With one hand he checked her step forward to get into the van, and with the other he wrenched the passenger door wide, and said crisply to Gio, 'This net of balls is too big to go in my car. You take it back to the circus in the van, and I'll bring Cara behind you in the car.'

'Cara's coming in the van with me. She belongs to me,' Gio shouted back at him furiously.

'Cara belongs to no one but herself. She told me so,' Tyler retorted, and before Gio could collect his wits sufficiently to reply, he dumped the net of balls into the passenger seat, slammed the door on them, and led Cara way to where his Jaguar was parked nearby.

'There's masses of room in your car,' she gasped, half laughing, half indignant at his effrontery. 'There's enough space in here for three times the number of balls in that net.'

'Do you want to be shouted at, all the way back to the circus?' Tyler asked her with a keen look.

'No.'

'Then get in.'

Cara got in, while Tyler held open the door for her, and waited courteously to see her settled in her seat before he joined her in the front, and observed calmly, 'Your partner will lose his licence if he continues to drive like that.'

The circus van, with Gio at the wheel, screeched out of its parking slot, the brakes slamming on as it reached the exit at the road, from where it roared away, heading out of town as if it were being pursued.

'He could have waited for us. I told him we'd follow on behind,' Tyler said mildly, and Cara shot him an amazed look.

'You knew very well Gio wouldn't wait, after what you just did,' she accused him.

She wanted to feel angry with Tyler. To shout at him

herself, for storing up trouble for her when she eventually got back to the circus, and a partner who was seething with temper.

Instead, her eyes met the twin devils dancing in Tyler's tawny orbs, and the crinkle of laughter that creased attractively round them, and a bubble of mirth inside her broke surface, and she was lost.

'You deserve to be spanked,' she gurgled, and lay back in her seat and wiped tears of laughter from her cheeks.

'What are you doing tomorrow?' Tyler asked unexpectedly when they left the traffic behind, and the road opened up clear in front of them.

Cara shot him a wary look. 'There are the usual morning chores, and then the service in the big top. If you want to talk to Uncle Mitch about the Falabellas, he'll be free after the service, I think,' she suggested with suddenly quickened breathing.

'I asked what *you* were doing, not Mitch,' Tyler retorted, and quickened her breathing still further.

'Oh. I, er . . .' Cara searched her mind frantically, and found it devoid of suggestions.

'That means you'll be free to come with me to London,' Tyler cut her short calmly.

'I didn't say . . .'

'Then you aren't doing anything that matters.' His lips lifted at her indignant gasp, and he said, 'Stop trying to think up excuses, and listen.'

He slowed the car to a crawl to pass two children on ponies, and when he was able to accelerate again, he resumed,

'I've got to go to the television studios in London tomorrow. They're running through the film of my last photographic expedition, along with the tapes of narrative of the script which I sent to them the other day. You'll enjoy it. I'll pick you up after the service in the big top. It isn't a very interesting journey into town, but it'll only take a little over an hour once we get on to the motorway, and when we've seen the run-through of the film, we can have lunch together somewhere, and a walk in one of the parks before we start back.'

'Is that why you asked me to come with you? Because it isn't a very interesting journey into town?' Cara shot back, and Tyler's smile widened, and he sent her a quizzical, sideways look.

'We could make it a lot more interesting, between us,' he suggested provocatively, and Cara's eyes snapped.

'In that case, you'll have to resign yourself to being bored,' she told him sweetly. 'I've got other things to do.'

'Such as?'

'Such as smoothing Gio's ruffled feathers, after the trouble you've caused today,' Cara retorted feelingly.

'If I thought Gio might . . .' Tyler ground, and the knuckles of his fingers momentarily showed white against the black rim of the steering-wheel.

'He won't. Uncle Mitch is quite capable of keeping Gio in order, without your help,' Cara answered, and added for good measure to annoy him, 'Not that I need either. I can handle Gio. He isn't the wolf he'd like to appear to be,' and hoped fervently it was not an empty boast.

'You look a little bit like Red Riding Hood yourself, in that track-suit,' Tyler teased, and her heart did a silly flip over, and forgot about Gio.

'Little Red Riding Hood was afraid of the wolf,' she returned tritely, and sat very still in her seat.

'Are you afraid?'

'It depends upon the wolf.'

She *was* afraid. Suddenly, inexplicably afraid, but of Tyler, not of Gio. And of herself, as much as Tyler. Her heart began to hammer, slow, painful strokes that caused a stoppage in her throat.

'I wonder which wolf is the more likely to eat you,' Tyler drawled, and gave a deep-throated chuckle when she moved convulsively away from him, in a movement she could not control, to the furthest edge of her seat.

'It depends on which one is the hungrier. Drop me off here, at the Park gates. I don't want to be taken right to my van,' she demanded shakily.

She groped for the door handle with fumbling fingers as the car slowed to a halt. Her heart was turning more somersaults than she had done herself in the store, and its antics made her feel dizzy.

The car seemed suddenly to be devoid of air, and if she did not get out quickly she felt as if she might faint. She snapped free of the seat-belt as if even that small confinement restricted the flow of oxygen.

Tyler leaned across, and his lips brushed lightly over her mouth. Cara went deathly still, as if she were turned to stone. 'I'm hungry for your company tomorrow, *Cara mia*,' he murmured persuasively, and his hands slid up behind her shoulders to turn her to face him.

'No!'

Quick as a flash, Cara's groping fingers closed on the door handle, and she pushed it open and ducked away from Tyler's grasp, and scrambled out of the car.

'No what, Cara?'

With quicksilver speed, Tyler was beside her. He slid across the two seats, and stood on the grass with her before she was even aware he had moved. She backed away from him, watching him with wary eyes.

'No, I won't come with you tomorrow,' she answered defiantly.

His eyes narrowed. 'Because you don't want to? Or because of Gio?'

'I'm busy. I . . . I shan't have time.'

'Busy doing what? The big top's closed for the winter now, so you don't have to prepare for any more performances. And the fairground booths don't have to be at the Hall until Tuesday. In any case, the men will have to attend to those. All you'll have to do is to tell Mitch what's required, and he'll see to the rest.'

All the while he was speaking, in a soft, slow, cajoling voice, Tyler had been inching unnoticed steadily nearer to Cara. How near, she was not aware until his arm shot out and pinioned her.

She gasped, and tried to spin out of his hold, but his hand curled round her waist, trapping her neatly against him. He had been stalking her, she realised furiously, with the deadly expertise of an accomplished hunter stalking his quarry. It was a tactic he must have honed to perfection in years of field work, and he now used it with equal and humiliating success against herself.

He reached out his other arm, and linked long fingers behind her back, and said smoothly, 'That only leaves washing your hair, or having a headache.'

'You seem to know all the classic excuses,' Cara flashed. 'You must have had lots of practice.'

A vision of jade-green loveliness flashed through her mind, and she strained away from him, trying to break his hold.

'Oh, lots,' he mocked. 'But think of all the advantages. When you know the tactics used by the other side, you're already half-way to out-manoeuvring them.'

He pulled her closer, trapping her arms against her sides so that she could not struggle, and helplessly her head fell back, and she looked up into his lean, tanned face. Her hair drifted away from her face, framing it like a pale flower against the black, silky strands. An errant wind blew one across her eyes, and Tyler raised his one hand and brushed it gently out of the way.

She quivered to his touch. His head bent above her, close, and closer, blotting out the sky. 'Is it worth carrying on fighting, *Cara mia*?' he asked her softly.

His mouth covered her own so that she could not answer him. She tried to twist her face away, but his fingers, riffling through her silky hair, held it fast, the hair she had washed only last night anyway. The faint perfume of the shampoo still clung to its shining darkness, and the feel of Tyler's fingers, combing, smoothing, stroking, sent electric thrills stabbing through to the very end of each strand.

His lips beguiled the corners of her mouth, demanding her surrender. His fingers played through her hair, gentling, soothing, undermining her resistance. With mounting panic, Cara felt herself begin to weaken.

In just the same way as the little stallion had weakened to the very same caresses. The comparison rankled, stiffening her against him.

'London can be lovely, even in November,' he coaxed.

London was probably where the photograph on the front cover of the magazine had been taken.

He wanted her to go with him, because the journey was a boring one, and any distraction was better than none.

Ask yourself if you're in the same league . . .

The weakness fled, and furious anger flooded through Cara. Sensing her unwilling response, Tyler's arms had loosened their hold, and she exploded like a fire cracker inside their circle. Exerting a strength she did not know she possessed, she burst away from him, her eyes flashing.

'I won't come with you,' she shouted. 'I won't, because I don't want to. Not because I'm busy. You can go to London on your own, and be bored to tears for all I care.'

'Don't want to, or don't dare to?' Tyler taunted, and ignored her outraged ejaculation. 'You're lovelier than ever when you're angry, *Cara mia*,' he grinned, and tacked on swiftly before she could speak, 'Put on something pretty tomorrow morning. I'll call for you after the service is over.'

'You . . . you . . .'

She vented her fury on empty air. The Jaguar slid away with a well-bred purr of its engine, and disappeared along the Park drive, and Cara was left with the sound of Tyler's mocking, 'See you tomorrow,' ringing in her ears.

Her mind churned as she hurried into the circus camp. The van was back, parked in its usual place, which meant Gio would not be far away. Probably watching for her to return, the same as he always did.

Had he seen Tyler kiss her?

Cara felt a prick of apprehension as her eyes searched the camp. So much for her boast that she could handle Gio. In her present mixed-up state, she did not feel capable of handling anyone, least of all herself.

Questions and unsatisfactory answers chased one another through her bewildered mind, and she sighed wearily as she headed towards her van, hoping that she might be allowed to reach its privacy before Gio spotted her.

She was nearly there when her partner appeared at the opening of the big top. His face was livid, and it was evident that he had seen Tyler kiss her. The moment he set eyes on Cara, he began to run towards her.

'Cara, do come and help me, there's a dear.' Her aunt had seen her too, and came to the door of her van to plead, 'The Wallace family are coming for the evening, and I'm all behind. I need some help with the baking.'

Despising herself for her cowardice, Cara scuttled up the steps of her aunt's van like a rabbit bolting for the safety of its burrow, and Gio stopped in his tracks, foiled. The confrontation with him was only postponed, Cara knew, but by tomorrow morning his temper would have had time to cool, and she would be in better control of herself as well, and hopefully she would manage to smooth things over again, she told herself without much conviction.

Cara remained with her aunt, and out of Gio's reach, for the rest of the afternoon. She mixed and baked and cut sandwiches, and only when she espied her partner holding one end of a heavy piece of equipment for some of the other circus men did she retreat to her van to change.

While they worked, Gio would not be able to loose his end, and hastily Cara used the time to slip into a scarlet woollen dirndl skirt and a white, high-necked sweater, and her mood lightened to match her clothes as she slid a scarlet bracelet on her arm, and hurried back to her aunt's van before Gio was free to move.

His glare followed her retreat, but Cara was too busy attending to the laden tea-table to worry about it, and when the Wallace family arrived shortly afterwards, they demanded her whole attention.

They were a cheerfully exuberant group. Mr Wallace was the quiet one, but his voluble wife more than made up for his lack, and the two sons, slightly older than Cara, and the daughter of her own age, kept her laughing with their anecdotes on the happenings in the fair during the two years since she had seen them last.

Carefully, no one mentioned Gio. Not even Mrs Wallace.

A hard-fought game of Monopoly took the party well into the night hours, and after a pick-where-you-please supper, and final drinks all round, it was nearly two o'clock in the morning before the visitors called their good nights, and wandered happily back towards their own camp.

Cara knew she was safe from a visit from Gio to her van at this late hour. Mitcham Brook's stern circus discipline was something that not even her partner in his present mood would dare to break.

Contrary to her expectations, Cara slept well. Nervous exhaustion took its toll, and the antidote of the Wallace family's cheerful company relaxed her sufficiently so that she fell asleep the moment her head touched the pillow, and woke early with a strange feeling of anticipation that she decided must be reaction to the bright sunshine after the week of heavy rain.

She felt rested and refreshed, and in control of herself again, and the bogey of the coming confrontation with Gio assumed more rational proportions than it had presented to her overwrought nerves the day before.

Gio could no longer pose a physical threat, she told herself jauntily. They had given their last trapeze performance together yesterday for the rest of the winter. She need not go aloft with him again until they started to practise before they went on the road again next Easter. That was several months away, and by that time all the fuss would have blown over, and the routine of being on the road once more would knit them together as a team, the same as before.

Instead of cheering her up, as it was meant to do, the thought brought with it a chill depression that took the brightness out of the morning, and drove her into a warm suit ready for the service in the big top.

The outfit was an extravagance she had picked up during their journey through Italy in the spring. It was in finely woven wool and cashmere, in palest cream, with a wide black patent-leather belt buckled round her slim waist.

The daintily frilled shell-pink blouse, the black patent handbag and court shoes came from the same source, and Cara surveyed the results in her mirror and felt better.

'Now to sort out Gio,' she muttered, and giving her hair a final pat for reassurance, she squared her shoulders, and marched down the van steps.

Gio met her at the bottom.

One look at his face warned Cara that her partner would not be sorted out so easily as she had imagined. Her lips compressed at the sight of him.

'You've been drinking,' she accused him bluntly.

'What if I have?' Gio wanted to know truculently.

'But you never drink.' Alarm began to stir in Cara.

Gio's face was blotchy, his stance far from steady, and from the sullen glare in his eyes it was obvious that he had spent a good part of the night fuelling the fire of his resentment. His mood looked frankly ugly.

'There's always a first time,' he mouthed.

'From the effect it's having on you, you'd better not drink any more,' Cara warned him sharply.

'And who'll stop me?' Gio sneered. 'You? Or that fancy boyfriend of yours? I want to talk to you about him.'

'Well, I don't,' Cara retorted. 'In fact, I don't want to talk to you at all while you're in this state.' She turned away in disgust.

'You're going to talk to me now, whether you like it or not. You've got a lot of explaining to do.'

Gio had not drunk sufficient to make him miss, when his hand shot out and grasped Cara by the wrist. She cried out shrilly as his fingers closed over her arm with a merciless grip.

'You're hurting me.'

'I'll hurt you a lot more before I'm through,' Gio snarled. 'I warned you. I'm warning you now, for the last time. You're mine.'

'I'm not yours. I'm not anybody's,' Cara denied furiously, and strove to pull away from the agonising grip.

'I'll make you mine, and then your boyfriend won't want to ever touch you again,' Gio shouted.

His face leered into Cara's, and she shrank back from

his whisky-laden breath, but his grip on her arm
increased, and he pulled her remorselessly with him
towards the open door of his living-van.

'Gio, don't. You're hurting my arm. Gio . . .'

'Loose her,' Tyler ordered coldly.

His words sounded like the crack of a pistol shot, and
his hand dropped heavily on to Gio's shoulder,
spinning him round. In his unsteady condition it rocked
the trapeze man off balance, and his arms flailed wildly,
loosing his grip on Cara in a desperate bid to save
himself from falling.

She staggered backwards, her eyes dilated, rubbing
the agony of her bruised wrist, and watching in
amazement as Tyler caught Gio by his scruff and his
seat, and hauled him bodily up the steps of his living-
van like a sack of potatoes. With a mighty swing of his
arms, he heaved the luckless trapeze artist inside, and
slammed the door.

'What's going on?' Mitcham Brook came running up
as Tyler descended the van steps, brushing his hands
together significantly.

'Your trapeze artist got above himself. I've just
brought him down to earth,' Tyler answered shortly,
and added with evident regret, 'I was strongly
tempted to make him pay for his behaviour, but the
man's too tipsy to be able to retaliate.' He sent Cara
a sweeping look. 'Did he hurt you?' His tone said he
might change his mind and punish Gio after all, if he
had hurt her.

Cara shook her head, unable to speak, and her uncle
filled in the gap forcefully.

'Leave Gio to me. I'll deal with him when he sobers
up. I don't warn any man twice.'

'He's your employee.' Tyler shrugged, turned to
Cara, and said in a tone that brooked no argument,
'You're coming with me, *now*. The further away you are
from the circus, the better, with what I think Mitch will
have to say to Gio.'

He took her by the arm and appraised her outfit.
'What you've got on will do nicely to travel in.' He
looked across at her uncle. 'I've got to go to the

television studios in London for a preview. I'll deliver her back here at about ten o'clock tonight. O.K.?'

Cara saw her uncle nod. She had time to feel surprised at the old-fashioned courtesy of Tyler asking her uncle's approval, and then not surprised, because it was Tyler, and he had a penchant for doing the unexpected. And then her hand was tucked firmly under his arm, and he was marching her towards the waiting Jaguar.

He put her into the passenger seat. Saw that her skirt was safely tucked in before he closed the door, and then joined her in the front. Her lips parted helplessly as she looked across at him, but no sound came, and before she could try again he said curtly, 'Belt up,' and with an inward giggle that threatened hysteria she wondered if it was an injunction to be quiet, or to fix the seat-belt round her.

Tyler's astringent tone had its effect, however, and Cara roused and locked the belt into place round her, then lay back in her seat as the car purred into life and nosed its way out of the circus camp.

A feeling of inevitability took hold of Cara. Tyler had said he would come, in spite of her refusal to go with him, and he had arrived, and she was with him now on her way to London. It was like being a puppet on a string, she thought helplessly. She rolled her head sideways on the seat, and looked up at him.

'Is your wrist really all right, Cara? Or would you like to go somewhere and have it checked?' he asked.

The sudden gentleness in his voice made her eyes prick, and she blinked rapidly to clear them, but Tyler's eyes were fixed on the road ahead, not looking at her.

'No, it isn't damaged. Only bruised,' she managed.

'Your partner's a savage.'

'He isn't like that usually.' Some innate loyalty made Cara defend the indefensible. 'Gio never drinks. Performers can't, you see, because they have to keep in perfect physical condition, so drinking and smoking are out. That's why it had such a dreadful effect on him.'

'I don't imagine Mitch will take such a soft-hearted view of Gio's behaviour,' Tyler gravelled. 'Gio will probably get his marching orders. At least, I hope he does.'

'Will that please you?' Cara asked wearily, and closed her eyes. Reaction was beginning to set in, and she suddenly felt drained. 'Gio's a top-rank trapeze artist. He'll be a loss to the circus. The irony of it is, he doesn't really want me. Only the circus. I was just the gateway to his ambitions, because I'm the only family Uncle Mitch has got.'

Tyler swore forcefully under his breath, and a muscle twitched at the corner of his jaw, ticking the pulse-beats away, but Cara's eyes remained closed, and she did not see.

She wondered vaguely what some other hapless driver must have done wrong, to make Tyler swear. He had not done so in her hearing before. But there was no sound of any other car passing them on the road, and her eyelids felt too heavy to open and allow her to look.

She slept.

CHAPTER EIGHT

CARA roused as the car braked to a halt.

'Are we here already?' She sat up, and looked confusedly round her.

'If by here, you mean the television studios, no,' Tyler answered. 'We're at a motorway café. We haven't got far to go now, but I thought it would be a good idea to have a coffee and a break before we get to London. It'll give you time to wake up.'

His eyes rested on her face as he helped her out of the car. The cool air nipped her cheeks, bringing back a faint colour to tinge their pallor, and he nodded as if satisfied as he led her into the café.

Cara's colour deepened when she sat down opposite to him at the table, and remembered the circumstances in which they had started their journey.

'I—I suppose I ought to thank you for—for ...' Embarrassment ground her to a halt.

'For saving you from a fate worse than death?' Tyler's voice was deliberately light, but his eyes were agate-hard as they glinted across the table. 'I just happened to come up at the right moment,' he disclaimed. 'Mitch and a couple of the circus hands were already running across to deal with Gio. I beat them to it, that's all. From the look on those men's faces, it'll go hard with your partner when he has to account for his behaviour,' he observed grimly.

'Don't,' Cara begged.

'Put him out of your mind,' Tyler ordered her briskly, his eyes on her receding colour. 'We'll be arriving at the studios in another half-hour, and when we get there I don't want anything to distract your attention from the film. It's in a different format this time from any we've done before, and it'll be useful to have your reaction.'

'Why mine?' Cara asked him bewilderedly. 'I'm no

authority on natural history films. I like watching them, of course, but . . .'

'You're a member of the general public, and it's the public's reaction that says whether a film's successful or not.'

Cara stared at him, her temporary gratitude evaporating. 'Is that why you brought me along with you this morning?' she cried. 'To test the temperature of public reaction? Using me, in fact, just the same as Gio?'

Tyler's face hardened at her words. 'Hardly with the same thing in mind,' he retorted abruptly, and Cara's face flamed, but it was anger this time that stained her cheeks, not embarrassment.

'Tell me what's the difference, in principle?' she invited him hotly.

Her sleep had refreshed her, but it had done little to calm her nerves. She felt strung up and edgy, and Tyler's calm assumption that he could use her as an opinion poll touched her on the raw.

Men were all alike, she thought bitterly. If they set their minds on something they drew you into their selfish schemes without a by-your-leave, and if you happened to object, that was just too bad.

Brooding, she sipped at her coffee, not wanting the drink, and yet not wanting to finish it and get back into the car with Tyler.

'Drink up,' he urged as the minutes ticked by, and the level in her cup showed no signs of sinking. 'We'll just make it to the studios if we go right away. Parking shouldn't be too difficult on a Sunday.'

'I don't want . . .' Cara began stubbornly, and Tyler interrupted in a voice that sharpened with impatience.

'The things you don't want seem to be legion. We've got an appointment.'

'*You've* got an appointment. I told you I wasn't coming. Remember?'

'And changed your mind afterwards,' Tyler sniped.

'You didn't give me any choice, this morning.'

'You've got a straight choice now,' Tyler returned flatly. 'I intend to be at the studios on time, with you or without you.' He paused to let the significance of what he said sink in, and then added for good measure, 'It's only about another half-hour's run in the car, but it'll be a very long walk, particularly in those shoes.'

His look took in the thin soles and high heels of her smart, patent-leather court shoes, and then his eyes returned to lock with her defiant stare. 'If you're thinking of hitching a lift on a lorry, forget it,' he said crisply. 'It's Sunday morning, and the heavy goods vehicles don't begin to roll until late tonight.'

'You . . .'

'Forget the names, as well,' he bade her crisply, 'and get into the car. I've got a reputation for being punctual, and I don't intend to break it now to satisfy your whims.'

He would rather break her instead.

The rest of the journey passed in a tight silence, and when after what seemed to Cara an age they at last drew into the studio car park, Tyler asked her abruptly,

'Are you coming in with me, or not?'

'It's too cold to sit out here.'

Cara was tempted to refuse, but the hour was still early, and she did not know how long Tyler was likely to be. The car park was only sparsely occupied, and he had parked the Jaguar facing a high brick wall, not the most inspiring view for solitary contemplation for what could be several hours. Inside the studios at least it would be warm, and presumably there would be other people to help ease the tension between them.

Huffily Cara preceded him through the big swing doors, and was startled at the hive of activity that greeted her inside.

The moment they appeared, a purposeful bustle caught them both along in its tide. It carried them from the smiling commissionaire, through innumerable doors, following a young man in shirt sleeves who hurried them along a bewildering maze of corridors, before passing them on to an older, more conservatively dressed man, who introduced himself as Mike.

Everybody seemed to know Tyler. Friendly greetings were called out to him from all sides, and a number of curious glances were sent in Cara's direction, but she was too busy trying to keep up with the fast pace set by their guide to notice.

'You're in Studio 4, Tyler,' their guide said.

He left them in the care of his colleague, and they walked through yet another door, this one emblazoned with the legend, 'Stud. 4'. It closed behind them, and the bustle ceased.

After the last hectic minutes, the silence was almost eerie. The studio was laid out in the form of a small cinema, Cara saw interestedly. A large screen took up one end of the room, and rows of comfortable-looking seats occupied the rest of the thickly carpeted area.

Carpeted, Tyler told her afterwards, not for the sake of luxury, but for the very practical purpose of sound deadening.

Mike ushered them to the front row of seats, and Cara sat down bemusedly. Tyler took the seat next to her, and the studio man the one on his other side. As soon as they were seated, Mike spoke to an invisible somebody, a disembodied voice answered back, and the lights went dim.

Immediately, a bright beam pierced the gloom, and the screen became alive.

'Come with me into another world . . .' The deep, cultured tones were so true to Tyler's normal speech that Cara turned, thinking he had spoken to her. But his lips were closed, his eyes intent on the screen, the dim light etching his face into a carved silhouette of perfect stillness.

The voice came from the tapes of narrative he had mentioned to her the other day, and the effect was uncanny, like having two Tylers with her in the studio at the same time.

One was more than she could cope with, she reflected ruefully, and dragged her eyes away from him, and back to the screen. To the other, wildlife world, as seen through the eyes of Tyler's camera. It was so different from, and yet so very much like, their own world, Cara thought with quick affinity.

Meeting, courting, and mating were there. Birth, and

growing up. And death, swift and violent, dealt out by a predator. The price of being free.

There was a price to be paid for everything, Cara thought bitterly, her heart wrenched with pity for the unfortunate water-buck.

The film rolled on, carrying her along with it, and Cara watched, enthralled. Unnoticed, her anger against Tyler melted, lost in the fascination of that other world. Tyler's world.

Narrative as such was almost non-existent. After the one brief opening, there were only the natural sounds of the wind and the wild. An occasional snatch of conversation between members of the team; the hissing of meat sizzling over an open brush fire. It was so real, Cara could almost smell the meat cooking, felt herself begin to drool with a devastating hunger honed by a long and arduous day in the field.

If this was Tyler's new format, it was brilliantly conceived and executed.

The shots were taken in such a way that the audience became the photographer, experiencing every thrill of discovery, every moment of disappointment and hardship, and breathtaking beauty.

Cara shivered with cold in a pre-dawn vigil, waiting for a wildcat to emerge from its lair. The soles of her feet winced at the scorching heat of sun-baked rocks, and she watched entranced as mewling lion-cubs stumbled about on buckling legs, their eyes scarcely yet open on the world they would one day dominate.

And when the rhinoceros charged, it was so real, so terrifying, that Cara jumped to her feet and screamed shrilly, 'Tyler! Look out . . .'

And knew, in that one brief second of irrational terror, that she loved him.

The knowledge was like a meteorite exploding inside her, sending cascades of brilliant light into all the dark, hidden corners of her consciousness, emblazoning the secret that had lurked there all along.

Her heart raced, sending a joyous singing through her veins. And then it contracted, and the brilliant sparkles faded like a November firework, leaving a deeper darkness behind them than she had ever known.

She loved Tyler.

But Tyler did not love her.

To him, she was merely a casual affair. An opportunist source of amusement to while away the long winter months until the circus left the Park again at Easter to return to their travels. Conveniently leaving the field clear for Tyler to resume his other interests.

Like the girl in the jade-green dress?

Cara's heart raced with suffocating speed, until it felt as if it must burst inside her. She swayed.

She became conscious of Tyler, on his feet beside her. Reaching out his hands to support her. Of Mike's voice, calling out something. And then the lights went up, and their plush surroundings reappeared, and the film lost its reality.

'Are you all right, Cara?' Tyler's voice sounded strained. She leaned against him, drawing on his strength.

Long shudders shook her body, and he cradled her against him until they ceased, and tremors of a different kind began to reach long fingers of bliss through her, radiating from his strong, encircling arms.

'Is she O.K., Tyler? Would you like a drink, Miss Varelli? A cup of tea, or perhaps something a bit stronger?'

Mike's voice, intruding on the bliss. Cara resented the voice, resented it drawing her back into the world that consisted of other people besides herself and Tyler. But the voice insisted, demanding to be answered. She drew in a deep breath, and reluctantly pushed away from Tyler's support, testing the strength of her legs.

She became aware of eyes watching her. Faces. Tyler's, and Mike's, and another man who was probably the projectionist. Embarrassment suffused her face.

'No, I'm fine. Truly I am. It was just that ... the picture was so real ... I—I got carried away,' she stammered. 'Oh, I do feel a fool. I'm so sorry,' she apologised abjectly.

'We'd better call it a day, Mike,' Tyler said, his eyes

still on her face, only half convinced by her
protestations. 'I can come back one day next week to
see the rest of the film.'

'No, you mustn't do that,' Cara protested immediately. 'I won't hear of it. You came all the way here to
see your film, and it isn't finished yet. Please, do go on.
I'd like to see it right through to the end myself. I
promise I won't be so silly again.'

She longed for the lights to go dim again, to hide her
burning face. To give her the privacy of darkness in
which to compose herself, and somehow come to terms
with the shattering new revelation that rocked her to the
very foundation of her being.

Mike looked at Tyler, and then back at Cara. 'If
you're sure . . .?'

'I'm positive. Please, Tyler.'

Her eyes pleaded with him. Pleading for darkness to
descend, to hide the threatened uprush of tears that any
moment now would dissolve her fragile strength.

Tyler looked at her for a long moment, an endless
moment when she dared not meet his eyes, and then
with a nod to the other man he drew her back to sit in
her seat beside him. The chair was deep, with thickly
padded arms which obliged him to remove his own
from about her waist, but he kept her hand clasped
comfortingly in his as they sat down, and the lights
dimmed again, and the film resumed its interrupted run.

The rhinoceros charged again, but this time it made
no impact upon Cara. Her thoughts were in a whirl.
The feel of Tyler's thumb absently stroking up and
down her wrist was a distraction that reduced the
activity on the screen to a blur of incomprehensible
noise and movement.

Cara watched it with unseeing eyes, aware only of
Tyler sitting in the seat next to her, leaning over
towards her the better to hold her hand, so close that
their shoulders touched. So close that, if she relaxed,
she could rest her head against his sleeve.

The girl in the jade-green dress was just the right
height to rest her head on his shoulder, if she had been
sitting in Cara's place.

As if by a process of thought transference, the girl herself appeared at that moment on the screen.

Cara stiffened, and then forced herself to relax. She was acutely conscious that Tyler's hand, closed round her own, must feel her every reaction. Which was what he had brought her here for, she reminded herself, using deliberate, self-inflicted cruelty to steady herself.

He would expect her to react to the shots of the animals. She had already done so, with humiliating effect. It would be even worse if she allowed herself to react to shots of the girl, and caused him to wonder why.

With a self-discipline that amazed her, Cara steeled herself to sit still and watch attentively as the girl on the screen attended to an injured fawn, the tiny creature's limpid eyes looking up trustingly into her lovely face as she bound its injured leg, then fed it from a bottle, an emotive scene calculated to catch the heart of any audience.

This time the girl was dressed in workmanlike garb of bush-shirt and slacks, her hair ruffled by the wind, and if anything it made her look even more beautiful than she had done on the cover of the magazine.

The contents of the bottle drained, the girl lifted the fawn in her arms and turned with a wide smile to look straight into the camera, and Cara became numbly aware of two things.

The girl's eyes were a clear, emerald-green.

And Tyler loosed her own hand, and smiled right back at her lovely likeness on the screen.

The lights went up, and Mike said in a satisfied voice, 'I think that shot of Rosemary and the fawn makes a good ending to the film. What do you think, Miss Varelli? She's a real enthusiast, isn't she?'

It would be so easy to ask, Who is she? But unaccountably Cara hesitated.

'I wouldn't know,' she said slowly. Suddenly, she did not want to. The pain of knowing the girl's name was enough, and her heart flinched from learning any more. 'We've never met.' She schooled her voice to steadiness. 'I saw her photograph with Tyler, of course, on the front cover of *Personalities*. It was the spring issue, I think,' she said carelessly.

'That's right,' Tyler agreed. 'The magazine sponsored a charity ball last March to benefit a conservation project we were involved in.'

No doubt Rosemary had been the belle of the ball, and Tyler her Prince Charming, Cara thought sourly, and turned blindly towards Mike who was saying, 'It was a good write-up they gave them, wasn't it?'

'Very good,' Cara agreed, and hoped fervently that Mike would not draw her into a discussion on the write-up, since her sole contact with the spring issue of *Personalities* had been its front cover, and the article inside the magazine was so much uncharted territory as far as she was concerned.

A pang pierced her at Mike's easy coupling of Tyler and Rosemary, accepting the two automatically as a pair. To her relief he spoke next to Tyler.

'I've booked a lunch at the Slade,' he said. 'I thought we could discuss the film while we fed. We'll be assured of a good meal there,' he grinned, 'we're doing a documentary on the hotel this afternoon, so if we go in your car, I could come back with the camera crew when we've got the film in the bag.'

It effectively postponed the time when Cara must be alone again with Tyler. A mixture of relief and resentment at Mike's intrusion jumbled her thoughts into even worse confusion as she tucked herself into the back seat of the Jaguar, using the excuse that it would give the two men more time to discuss the film if they sat in the front together.

The car slid smoothly into the traffic, and Cara sat behind Tyler, struggling to subdue the turbulence inside her so that, when the lunch was over and they were alone again together, she could face the journey back with at least an outward appearance of calm.

She studied the back of Tyler's neatly dressed head, rising with a proud lift from his broad shoulders, and wondered if Rosemary's fingers were ever afflicted with the urge that her own felt now, to smooth along the deep tawny waves that cleared his collar in an expertly barbered line.

She clenched her hands into fists in her lap, resisting the longing with all the strength she possessed. Wondered with a humourless smile what Mike would think if she succumbed and reached forward to stroke the back of Tyler's head. What Tyler himself would think.

Tyler must not know. Whatever happened, she must not give him any inkling of how she felt. She had not had time to get used to it herself, yet. Would she ever? she wondered unhappily.

It might be an interesting experiment to tame you . . .

His words returned to mock her. How well he had succeeded, only she knew. But at least she was spared the ultimate humiliation of Tyler knowing, too. From now on, whenever she was with him, she would have to guard her every look and gesture. How he would gloat over his success if he should discover her secret.

Cara cringed at the prospect, and recklessly accepted a large sherry while they waited for their order, and hoped that the unaccustomed alcohol would not have the same disastrous effect upon her as it had had on Gio.

It relaxed her sufficiently to allow her to make a pretence of enjoying the fabulous dishes which the waiter produced with a flourish to impress the television man.

Intricately presented starters, a main dish smothered with an exotic-tasting sauce, and a sumptuous sweet succeeded one another with smooth precision, but Cara toyed with the contents of her plates, managing to eat only enough to prevent open comment from her companions on her lack of appetite.

And when the plates were removed, she could not afterwards remember what it was she had eaten. Only that, however exotic, the offerings of the Slade could not even begin to compete with roast pheasant and tiny button sprouts fresh from the garden and raspberry soufflé, eaten in a small ante-room overlooking Broadwater Park.

Mike talked almost non-stop throughout the meal.

Cara watched him in amazement, wondering how it was he managed to swallow any food at all, with scarcely a break between words.

Both men were perfectionists in their own field, she discovered, listening to their conversation. By the time the meal reached the coffee stage, they had dissected and fitted together again almost every inch of the film they had just watched, until Cara wondered bewilderedly if they could find anything at all to satisfy them in what she herself had thought to be a perfect production.

Technicalities of presentation and timing flowed back and forth across the table, and Cara refused a second cup of coffee and slipped away to the ladies' room to freshen up, feeling forlornly that if she did not come back for the next hour, she would not be missed.

Tyler was alone when she returned.

'Mike sends his adieus and apologies,' he explained the absence of the television man. 'The camera crew arrived early, and they've hit an unexpected complication with the filming that only he can sort out, apparently, so he couldn't wait.'

'Mike seems to thrive on difficulties,' Cara returned tartly. 'If he can't find any genuine ones, he invents them. I don't think there was a single shot in your film that he didn't pull to pieces.'

She was startled by the fierce resentment that burned inside her, that anyone should dare to criticise Tyler's work.

Be careful. Remember. He must not suspect.

'On the contrary, Mike was delighted with it,' Tyler contradicted. 'But in television, the timing has to be so slick there's no margin for error. The old adage of "it'll be all right on the night" simply won't wash in television. Every single detail has to be hammered out beforehand.'

'Hammered being the operative word,' Cara remarked sourly, refusing to be convinced.

'You'll see the difference when the film's presented on your screen next year,' Tyler told her confidently. 'Judging from your own reaction, Mike reckons he's got an award winner on his hands.'

'Don't,' Cara groaned.

'No, he means it. He says it'll get the audience on its feet.'

'It got me on my feet,' Cara flashed back, stung into anger at Tyler's callous indifference to her feelings. 'I don't think it was funny.'

'You made a lovely barometer,' he grinned.

'It was a cruel thing to do. Cruel, and mean. You knew what was coming, and you deliberately didn't warn me. You just sat there, and let me be frightened out of my wits to suit your own selfish purpose.'

Cara felt perilously close to tears. She hated Tyler for what he had done to her, and wondered raggedly how you could love someone and hate them at the same time.

'Nonsense.' His voice crisped. 'You over-reacted, that's all. That scene with Gio this morning upset you.'

'So it's my fault now.'

'I didn't say that.' His tone was edged with impatience. 'Come and have a stroll in Hyde Park, and calm down. We'll walk our lunch off before we start back.'

He rose and hooked his sheepskin jacket carelessly over one shoulder, and tucking her hand under his other arm he drew her to the door. For a moment Cara rebelled, but only for a moment. She did not want to walk in Hyde Park. But neither did she want to get straight back into the car, and face an enclosed hour with Tyler on the ride back.

Her jangled nerves recoiled from another fraught journey, and she wanted to cling to the presence of other people for as long as possible.

Tyler mistook her hesitation. 'It isn't far to the park. Speakers' Corner is only just along this road.'

The usual conglomeration of speakers harangued the strolling Sunday crowd, and one livelier than the rest drew a reluctant laugh from Cara as they paused to listen. The laugh lightened Cara's black mood, and they moved on to stroll beside the Serpentine.

It was cool beside the water, with a light wind ruffling the surface into tiny waves, and in spite of her wool suit Cara shivered.

'Have my sheepskin over your shoulders. It'll keep the wind out.'

Tyler unhooked his finger from the chain at the back of the jacket collar, and slipped it on to her, sliding her arms into the sleeves for extra warmth.

'You might want it for yourself,' she objected.

'My suit jacket's thicker than yours, even if it isn't so becoming,' he smiled. 'I brought the sheepskin from the car in case you might need it.'

With deft fingers he turned up the collar, framing her face like a flower against the curly white fleece. 'It almost makes an overcoat on you, you're so tiny,' he teased.

It was just a jacket on Tyler, but it reached almost to Cara's knees, and she snuggled into it gratefully, warmer because it was Tyler's coat, the garment that had moulded its soft shape to his body, and now caressed her own.

Surreptitiously Cara grasped the fleece and pulled it closer round her, savouring the faint male smell that clung to it, and marked it peculiarly his own.

'Is it slipping off you?'

His alert eyes noticed her movement and misinterpreted it, and he slid his arm across her shoulders and grasped the coat, and held it against her, and Cara thrilled to the pressure that drew her closer to his side.

Other couples strolled arm in arm beside the water, taking advantage of the fine weather while it lasted. She and Tyler must look just the same as those other couples, Cara mused. But the likeness was only on the surface. Her heart twisted at the difference.

She wondered if he had brought Rosemary walking in Hyde Park. He had taken her to a ball, to dance the night away together, and then afterwards he would tuck the long, jade-green dress carefully into the front seat of the Jaguar, and he would see her home, and . . .

Pain stabbed through her at the contrast, and dimly she became aware that Tyler was speaking to her.

'We'll walk as far as Peter Pan's statue, and then go back. You must have something to eat before we start for home.'

Home. Could any contrast be greater? Cara asked herself bleakly.

'It isn't long since we had lunch.' She was not hungry for food, only for Tyler, and her heart faced famine, and was afraid.

'You scarcely touched your meal at lunchtime.'

So he had noticed. Perhaps he would blame the cause on the upset in the studio. Perhaps, in part, it was.

Cara stood with Tyler and gazed at the world-famous statue, and envied the eternal child that Barrie had created. Relationships for children were so simple. Unquestioning. Uncomplicated. Just plain black and white, with none of the overlapping shades of grey that continually threatened the peace of adulthood.

Unconsciously Cara sighed, and Tyler said contritely, 'I shouldn't have walked you so far. You've had a long day. I know of a place not far from here that provides a nice tea.'

He could not guess how long a day it had been for Cara. A lifetime of self-discovery long, and once it had been lived, there could be no going back.

A bewildering maze of streets replaced the green, and Tyler turned her through a door into a small café, unpretentious on the outside, but inside shining with cleanliness, and crowded with devotees.

Someone made room for them on a corner bench, and they squashed up together. The long sleeves of the sheepskin jacket, so cosy over her finger ends in the park, rendered Cara handless now, and Tyler laughed at her predicament, and rolled back one sleeve for her into a thick woolly cuff, to enable her to eat the café speciality of hot buttered muffins.

He shook out a spotless lawn handkerchief from his top pocket, and gave it to her to wipe off the butter oozing over her chin, and coaxed her to eat yet one more until he was satisfied that she was filled.

The available room on the bench was so small that Tyler ate one-handed himself, and kept his other arm round Cara to prevent her from slipping off the seat, pulling her half on to his lap to make her more comfortable.

'You make a nice easy chair,' she managed shakily, and tried in vain to stop her heart from doing crazy somersaults inside her breast.

'You'll have to sit there more often,' his voice teased her ear, and set her heart off on another exercise that made it almost impossible for her to swallow the food she was eating.

The simple fare was nectar, but when a departing customer left room on the bench, and Tyler released her to sit more freely, the rich plum cake and hot strong tea that followed lost their flavour.

Tyler was silent as they started the journey back.

He took the sheepskin jacket from Cara and slung it on to the back seat of the car, and said, 'You won't need that now. It'll be warm in the car.' And she felt herself bereft, with a coldness inside her that was the chill of returning reality, and had nothing to do with the temperature of the night.

It was very dark. Heavy clouds rolled across the sky with the sunset, and obscured any light from the moon. The Jaguar's powerful headlights cut a wide white swathe in front of them, making the blackness on either side even darker by contrast.

It seeped into her spirits as the car rolled the miles smoothly behind them, each one passed bringing them closer to the circus. Cara thought about Gio. She did not want to, but it was easier than thinking about Tyler. Or Rosemary. Gio had no power to hurt her.

They left the motorway, and the lights of a small town lay directly ahead of them. Broadwater. They were nearly home. Cara stirred uneasily in her seat.

Tyler said, 'You were so quiet, I thought you were asleep.'

He swung the car into an empty layby, and switched off the engine and the lights, and the darkness crowded into the car, shutting them in. Cara heard two clicks, and felt her seat belt snake across her body, releasing her. She put up her hand to hold it back, but it slipped through her fingers in the darkness and was gone. And then Tyler's fingers came and took her by the chin, and turned her face towards him.

'Are you glad, now, that you came with me?' he asked her softly.

'I . . .' She stopped. She did not know whether she felt glad, or sorry.

She hardly felt anything, except his fingers cupping round her chin, turning her thoughts to helpless confusion, and her muscles to water. If she had stayed behind, how long would it have taken before she realised she loved him? she wondered bemusedly. Days? Weeks?

'I didn't have any option,' she prevaricated.

'So, I hijacked you, and then frightened you half to death.' His voice was close, a teasing murmur. 'Was it so terrible?'

Not half so terrible as the things his lips started to do to her mouth. They explored its shape with a slow, lazy enjoyment that sent arrows of sensation shafting through her body. Mad, crazy arrows, pricking every nerve into throbbing life.

His lips continued their journey down the slender column of her throat, and found the wildly beating pulse in the scented hollow at its base. Cara's hands came up, weak hands with only the strength in them to creep round the back of his neck to stroke his hair, giving in to the impulse that they had managed to resist while Mike was with them in the car.

Tyler felt her touch, and his kiss intensified, grew more demanding. The warnings she had given herself fled, and her lips pursed in passionate response, exchanging kiss for kiss.

'I didn't mean you to be frightened, *Cara mia*,' Tyler whispered huskily, straining her closer.

'Don't call me that. I've told you before . . .'

Cara pulled away from him, stung by the hated phrase. It was a favourite expression of Gio's, and when he used it, it was a term of possession, not endearment. On Tyler's lips it became a mockery. She was not his. She would never be his. On his own admission, she was merely 'an interesting experiment'. His very words. They came back to her with bitter clarity.

'Why not? What's wrong with it? Is it Gio's pet name

for you, perhaps?' His tone became a taunt. 'Is that why you hate it, because of him?'

'I don't hate Gio.'

Deliberately Cara sidestepped his question, using Gio's name as a shield against him. Against the force of her own wayward emotions, which threatened to betray her secret to his searching lips if she could not escape them soon, and stop the torture that was twisting her heart in two.

She felt Tyler withdraw, and it was like a physical blow. She flinched in the darkness, and heard him exclaim,

'I shall never understand women!'

He was not alone in that respect, Cara thought without humour. Women did not understand themselves. She sent him a barbed,

'Not after all the practice you must have had?'

'Maybe I'm a slow learner.'

His tone bit. His arms dropped away from her, and Cara shrank back into her seat. The lights of a passing car lit up the planes of his face, granite hard, and unsmiling. His hands moved. There was a click as his seat belt locked into position, and slowly Cara reached out and pulled her own belt across.

Tyler waited until he heard the metallic sound of the lock before he keyed the engine into life. He flicked a switch and the headlights blazed on, and the car swung out of the layby and back on to the road towards Broadwater and the circus, and inside it, tension gripped the air between them, as brittle as when the journey started.

Except that now it was Rosemary, and not Gio, who occupied Cara's thoughts. The image of the green-eyed girl she had seen on the screen hovered like a wraith across her mind.

Tyler could not be still learning about Rosemary. The message in the girl's smile as she turned to the camera—and to Tyler behind it—was one of total rapport between them, amply confirmed by the softness of his smile as he looked back at her lovely image on the screen.

Rosemary. A sweet, old-fashioned, typically English name. The complete antithesis of her own. It fitted in perfectly with Tyler and his background.

They were both in the same league.

CHAPTER NINE

Gio had already left when Cara returned to the circus.

Disregarding her angry protests, Tyler took her right to the door of her uncle's van instead of to her own, and insisted upon seeing her inside, and into her relatives' care, before refusing their offer of supper, and returning almost immediately to his car.

He did not attempt to touch her again after they left the layby. In fact, he hardly spoke to her at all, except to refuse her request to drop her at the Park gates, but his piercing glance, and his 'See you on Tuesday,' as he left, were sharp reminders that she could not hope to escape him for long.

'I've sacked him,' Mitcham Brook told her briefly when Cara broached the subject of Gio.

'Was that necessary?' she asked wearily. 'It'll mean endless trouble, getting another trapeze man, and co-ordinating our act together.'

'You couldn't trust yourself aloft with Gio again. I wouldn't allow it,' her uncle said adamantly. 'I've already made a few phone calls, putting out feelers for another trapeze man, so you needn't worry about that either,' he said, his eyes on her puckered brow. 'Now I'm off to make my rounds.'

He kissed Cara good night with more than his usual tenderness, and she looked helplessly across at her aunt as the door closed behind him.

'I wish it hadn't happened this way,' she sighed. 'Was it very bad, this morning after I left?'

'No. I think Gio realised he was getting off lightly,' Beth replied. 'Feeling among the circus hands was running high, and if Gio had attempted to make a scene, it would have gone hard with him, and he knew it.'

She spooned Ovaltine into two mugs of hot milk, and pushed one across the table to Cara.

'Linda's gone, as well,' she announced quietly.

'Linda? Oh, no! Now we're two performers short,' Cara groaned. 'And it's all my fault.'

'Of course it isn't,' her aunt scolded gently. 'Gio wanted to marry you, and you didn't want to marry him. It's silly to blame yourself for that. You can't bind yourself for the rest of your life to an unsuitable partner, just for the sake of keeping the peace.'

'I suppose Linda's gone after Gio? She wanted him.'

'She's welcome to him,' her aunt snorted. 'Linda tried to create a scene before she left, but Poppy soon put a stop to that, and she went off in a huff, and good riddance. I never did like her. She's a mischievous creature.'

'That's all very well,' Cara frowned, 'but Linda was due to do a juggling act at the Hall on Tuesday. How am I going to explain to Tyler?'

'There's no need to,' her aunt smiled complacently. 'Little Mario, Pepi's eldest, is stepping in to fill the slot. You know how good he's become with the clubs this summer, and what better than a child performer at a children's party? Seeing him perform will make all the other children want to try for themselves, and as for Mario, he's wild with excitement. He can't wait to show off to his new classmates,' she chuckled.

'You seem to have solved everything very nicely without my help,' Cara laughed, and kissing her aunt good night, she returned to her own van. But not to sleep.

Slow hours of restless tossing passed before she at last dropped into an uneasy doze, disturbed by wild dreams of a green-eyed rhinoceros that charged her again and again, getting larger and more ferocious each time, until she awoke with a cry to find herself fighting the sheets into a tangled mass on the bed.

Two gaps in the line of living-vans shouted at her as she emerged to groom and feed the horses, and she turned her back on them impatiently and took Pride and the dogs to the beach, lingering there for as long as possible rather than return to the circus, and her own unwelcome thoughts.

She saw nothing of Tyler on the shore. She did not want to, she told herself fiercely, and sternly repressed any thought that she had chosen the beach on which to exercise the animals on the off-chance that Tyler might decide to do the same.

When she returned to the camp her aunt called out to her, 'Cara, can you take this knitting pattern to Mrs Wallace? I promised to let her have it, but I've got a batch of cakes in the oven, and I can't leave them.'

The fair was to continue operating until the end of the week, and for the first time ever, Cara felt she would be glad to see them gone. The raucous music from the roundabouts grated on her over-stretched nerves as she made her way to the Wallaces' van, and she longed to press her palms over her ears to shut out the sound.

Oh Rose Marie, I love you, the music poured from the roundabouts.

It was only one of a variety of tunes that blared from the loudspeakers, and Cara had not noticed it particularly before, but now it hammered inside her head with a dreadful persistence that she felt must slowly drive her mad.

Rose Marie. Rosemary. Why did the two names have to be so alike?

'Can't you stop the thing, even for a few minutes?' she protested in desperation to an astonished Mrs Wallace. 'Surely you've got some modern music? Pop records, or something?' she defended her eccentric request, unable to explain why she suddenly hated the lovely old ballad.

'Modern music doesn't fit in with the pace of the hobby-horses, dearie.' Mrs Wallace told her what Cara already knew, and she pushed the knitting pattern into the older woman's hand, and fled as the latter began to hum off key, *'Oh Rose Marie, I love you. I'm always dreaming of you.'*

How long did it take for a breaking heart to stop beating? Cara wondered despairingly. She did not fit with Tyler, either. Rosemary did. Whatever the green-eyed girl was to Tyler, there was no doubt that she fitted.

No matter what I do, I can't forget you ... the hurdy-gurdy wailed on, searching Cara out as she ran quivering into her van, and continued to pursue her through the loudly slammed door,

Sometimes I wish that I had never met you ...

If only she had not met Tyler.

Cara dropped her face into her shaking hands, and felt slow tears begin to trickle through her fingers. If she had not met Tyler, she would still be her own person. Now, whether he wanted her or not, she belonged to him. Her heart would never be wholly her own again.

If she had not met Tyler, she might even, by now, have accepted the inevitability of being married, at some time in the future, to Gio.

And she would have missed the heartache, and the bliss, of being in Tyler's arms. Of feeling his lips on her own. Which was all she would have to take with her into the future.

The next morning, Ben called her over as he loaded the apparatus into the van, ready to transport it to the Hall. 'Come with me, Cara,' he begged. 'You know the set-up there, and I don't. I don't particularly want to disturb Lord Broadwater or his agent, just to ask them where to put the bits of apparatus.'

Cara hesitated. Was there to be no reprieve for her? She had not planned to go to the Hall until the last possible moment for the performance that afternoon. But if she refused Ben, it would only invite comment.

'Wait a minute while I get my anorak,' she agreed reluctantly, and climbed into the vehicle beside the clown, zipping up her jacket as if it were an armour against Tyler.

Daniels met them half way along the Park drive, and slowed down his Range Rover to have a word with them.

'Go in and out of the Hall as you need to,' he told them helpfully. 'I've left the front doors open for you. If you want anything, ask Mrs Turner. She's busy in the kitchen.'

'Phew!' Ben whistled his awe as he surveyed the size

of the ballroom. 'This is a bit different from our living-vans, wouldn't you say?'

'Very,' Cara agreed drily. 'Put the apparatus in the corner near the door from the entrance hall. It'll be out of the way, and easy to get at when we come in to do our acts.'

There was no sign of Tyler.

Cara listened for the red setter's bark, when it sensed the presence of strangers in the house, but the place remained silent as they walked in and out, carrying the apparatus. The study door remained firmly closed. It drew Cara's eyes like a magnet each time she passed on her way to and from the ballroom.

Was Tyler sitting in the study behind it? she wondered. Perhaps listening to them coming and going, and deliberately ignoring their presence in his house?

If he was there, he could not but be aware of their activities. He was expecting them, and although they were as quiet as possible, the movement of even such a small amount of apparatus carried with it a share of noise.

Ben turned to pull the door to behind him, and dropped Pepi's metal table with a clatter, and Cara's eyes flew to the study door, but it remained still, and silent. And firmly closed.

It was a snub. An insult, to know that they were in his house, and not to come out to greet them, Cara fumed.

'That's the lot.' Ben checked the pile of apparatus. 'I must say, the decorations for the party look lovely. All that's needed now are the children.'

'They'll be here soon enough. And so shall we.' Cara urged Ben back outside, and climbed into the van with undisguised haste.

Through the windscreen, her eyes sought the library windows, but there was no sign of movement from behind the leaded panes, although it was possible that Tyler might be sitting further back into the room, out of sight from the drive, and watching them even now.

'Let's get going.' Cara hurried Ben into his seat, and the clown cast her a puzzled look.

'What's the hurry?' he protested. 'We've done everything we can until the show begins this afternoon. Why not take our time, and enjoy the fleshpots while we can?' he joked.

'We shall be in the way of the fairground lorry, when it comes to deliver the booths,' Cara exaggerated, and let out a silent breath of relief as Ben obediently set the van in motion, and drove it, and herself, out of sight of the library windows.

'I've arranged for us to be at the Hall half an hour before the children start to arrive,' she warned him, and left it as late as she possibly could before going to collect Poppy's Mexican costume in which to do the lasso-dancing.

The tight black trousers clung to her slender hips, topped by a full-sleeved white silk blouse, and a black bolero. Cara tipped the large black sombrero at a saucy angle on her head, and said with an attempt at bravado,

'I can't make any mistakes while I'm wearing your costume. It really makes me feel the part.'

Poppy ran critical eyes over her appearance. 'Thank goodness it doesn't need altering.'

'It shouldn't. I'm more or less your size.'

'You're more or less the size I used to be,' the clown's wife returned ruefully.

'Never mind. You'll be attending the party at the Hall yourself next year, complete with twins,' Cara comforted, and wondered bleakly what she herself would be doing then.

She did not think she could bear ever to come back to Broadwater. And yet the prospect of going away for good, and leaving nothing of herself behind, left her feeling unutterably depressed.

To become nothing but a faint memory to Tyler, and later on perhaps not even that.

On a sudden impulse she ran back to her van, and slipped the gold ball-point pen she had bought for her uncle into her bolero pocket. She would give it to Tyler instead. She did not give herself time to question how or when she would give it to him.

His own pen was broken, and it was not Christmas

yet, so he would not have another pen given to him as a
present before then. She would find some way to let him
have it, she assured herself. And long years hence, he
would use the pen to write his books and scripts with, and
she would have some small part in his future after all. The
thought was a comfort, if only a small one.

'Go and enjoy yourselves,' Poppy urged as she waved
them off. 'It should be fun, with all the children there.'

Cara and Ben took the circus contingent along with
them in the van. As they entered the imposing hall, the
children clung closely to her, awed by their surroundings, and Cara clung just as closely to them, her need of
moral support momentarily eclipsing their own, for a
different reason.

Tyler was in the library this time. The door was ajar,
and his voice came clearly through it, talking to
someone on the telephone.

'The preview of the film was great, Rosemary. I told
you, I took someone with me.'

Someone. He meant herself. Cara's feet froze to the
floor. She was so insignificant in Tyler's eyes that she
did not even warrant a name. Anger smouldered inside
her as Tyler's voice went on enthusiastically,

'The reaction was all we'd hoped for, and more.
We've backed a winner this time, love.'

Love. Cara's heart contracted. She herself had
backed a loser.

'Yes, fine,' Tyler's voice went on. 'It can't be too
soon for me. When does your plane land? Try and get
here for the party, if you can. Yes, I can't wait.'

A pause, and then Tyler laughed. A deep, teasing
laugh. He said,

'Not until the summer. It's easier to move around in
the bush after the rainy season's stopped. Why don't
you think about what I suggested, and turn it into a
combined honeymoon?'

Cara had heard enough. Too much. Her feet unfroze
from the floor, and she dragged Ben and the children
into the ballroom, away from the hateful study door,
and the sound of Tyler's soft laugh.

Laughing with Rosemary. Planning to combine their

honeymoon with their next safari in the summer.

All that she had wondered about since she first saw the green eyes turn to smile at Tyler from the screen crystallised into heart-wrenching certainty, and Cara wondered shudderingly how she could manage to live through the rest of the afternoon. Even perform in front of Rosemary, if she managed to reach the Hall early enough to join in the party.

Fervently, she wished it were herself, and not Linda, who had gone away. Not to join Gio. That was not a solution for her. But to hide, as a wounded creature hides, until the wounds had healed, and only the scars were left to remind her of the pain.

She *would* go away, she vowed. After this one performance, there was nothing to stop her from taking a holiday. The rest of the private bookings were of the clown-and-conjuror variety, that did not include herself, and she would be free to take a break without exciting comment.

Anywhere would do. It did not matter, so long as it was as far away as possible from Broadwater, and the danger of meeting Tyler. Or worse still, meeting Tyler and Rosemary.

He appeared in the ballroom as if in answer to her thoughts, and Cara felt herself go rigid. Her breathing seemed to stop as she watched his loose-limbed stride bring him across the floor towards them.

'Your outfit's very fetching,' he approved, his eyes wandering lazily over her costume.

The pen seemed to burn a hole in her bolero pocket. Cara found herself wondering irrationally if he would sense what it was that made the bulge in the soft material, and guess that it was meant for him.

'I've come instead of Linda. She's gone,' Mario piped up, and saved her.

'Linda's—er—indisposed,' Cara interrupted the child hurriedly, and added with a sharp warning glance at Mario, 'This is Pepi's eldest son. He's an expert juggler already, so we thought you wouldn't mind him coming along instead. It might even be more interesting for the children to see another child performing.'

She wished Tyler would look away. He seemed to be studying her spartan costume as if it were some rare, detailed tribal dress, she thought angrily, and felt herself flush hotly under his mocking surveillance.

'That sounds like some more arrivals.' Cara turned with relief as an excited chattering approached the outer door, and Daniels ushered in a small crowd of children.

'That's my cargo, safely delivered,' he said gratefully, coming up to join them.

'Aren't you collecting all of them?' Cara was not interested, but her tongue seemed to cleave to the roof of her mouth when she tried to talk to Tyler.

'Only the ones from the outlying farms,' Daniels answered. 'The others are meeting at the village school, and Tyler's provided a coach to collect them from there. It sounds as if they're just arriving. They'll be quieter than my lot. The teachers are travelling in the coach,' he grinned.

'I'd better go and meet them.' Tyler strolled away, and Cara relaxed.

'You can take it easy now, until it's time to play Father Christmas,' she smiled at Daniels.

'Oh, I'm not playing Father Christmas. Tyler is,' Daniels answered. 'He takes his position as host very seriously. Come and see his cloak,' he invited. 'He collected it this morning, while you were bringing in the apparatus.'

So that was where Tyler had been. He had not been in his study after all.

'It's long.' Cara's eyes widened as Daniels escorted her into a small room off the ballroom, where the red cloak and hood, with accompanying white cotton-wool whiskers and beard, hung in splendour.

'He had to have it specially made, because he's so tall. But it's a good investment. It should last him for years, for occasions like this.'

Cara winced at the thought of those future, happy years. Happy, that is, for Tyler and Rosemary.

'This is where all the action's been taking place.' Daniels excused the chaotic state of the room with an apologetic wave of his hand. 'There's the sack of presents, in that corner by the cloak. I've only just finished labelling them. I've left a few spare presents and labels still on the table, in case we get some unexpected extra children.'

'Mr Daniels, can you come for a minute? We need some more chairs. Oh, I'm sorry, Miss Varelli. I didn't know you were together.'

'That's all right, Mrs Turner,' Daniels assured the flustered-looking housekeeper. 'I'll come right away. Excuse me for a moment, while I sort out the crisis,' he smiled at Cara, and hurried off.

Cara's eyes flew to the table. It was littered with spare labels, and ball-point pens. In a moment she had drawn out a chair and sat down. All the labels were alike, with a picture on the front of a snowman with a bunch of holly. It would give her gift just the anonymity she needed, she thought with satisfaction.

Without giving herself time to think any more, in case she should lose courage, she wrote on the label, 'To Father Christmas, with love.' She hesitated for a moment over the words, 'with love', then dashed them off. She ignored the line marked, 'From ....'

She tugged the pen in its neat presentation case from out of her bolero pocket, tied the label firmly to it, and taped it to make it extra secure.

With a quick glance towards the door to make sure she was unobserved, she sped across to the corner, and tossed her gift into the sack of presents before she could change her mind. Then she gave the sack a good shake, so that the pen would slide down to the bottom.

It was a heaven-sent solution to her problem. This way, Tyler would have the pen, and he would never guess who it had come from. He would probably think that the children had made a collection to give it to him, to thank him for the party, and wanted to keep it a secret.

And he would use it, and probably treasure it, for that reason. And her secret would be safe.

She was just in time. 'I wish every problem were as simple to sort out as that one,' Daniels said as he rejoined her, and added, 'We're nearly ready for the performance to begin, if you are?'

'Whenever you say the word,' she answered.

Cara's heart was beating uncomfortably fast as she strolled back with Daniels into the ballroom. The headmistress of the local school smiled across at her, and Tyler turned from her side and came across to join Cara, leaving the teacher and her staff to get the children settled into their seats.

'What order are you bringing on the acts?' Tyler asked her.

'I thought the clown first, with the dogs, to break the ice.' Cara felt on safer ground, talking practicalities, and her voice was firm as she went on with more confidence, 'After that, Mario can come on and do his juggling act, then the magician.'

'And your lasso-dance?'

'That comes last, before teatime.'

'In that case, come and sit on the window-seat with me, and watch the others until it's time for your turn.'

She would have felt safer waiting at a distance, along with Pepi and Mario. Warning signals flashed in Cara's mind, and her heart began to thud uncomfortably again as Tyler's hand came up to cup her elbow, and draw her with him towards the low window-seat beside the rows of occupied chairs. One of the children's teachers moved her chair aside to give them room to pass, and with the low window-seat confronting her she had no time to think up an excuse.

'I'll sit behind you,' Tyler said. 'You can lean back on me, and watch the show in peace.'

He slid deep into the window embrasure and drew her down beside him, pulling her back across the polished wood, and pressing her against him. 'Comfortable?' he asked.

If leaning against red hot needles was comfortable, she supposed she must be. Electric currents flowed out from him, sending tongues of fire licking through her, curling her nerves into knots.

Cara's head rested just underneath Tyler's chin, and his mouth when he spoke brushed the tip of her left ear, burning it with a fierce pain. She stiffened sharply away from the contact, trying ineffectually to sit herself upright against the restraining pressure of his arm.

'Relax,' his voice mocked in her ear. 'There's no rhinoceros to charge us here, I shan't eat you. I prefer jelly.'

In that case, her legs would qualify. If they did not stop shaking, she would never be able to do her lasso-dance without getting hopelessly tangled up in the rope, and disgracing herself in front of her young audience.

But how to stop the trembling, when Tyler's arms moulded her body close to his? They curved her spine to the hard contours of his lean thighs, and brought her head to rest against his broad chest, through which throbbed the strong, even beat of his heart.

His heart that beat for Rosemary.

'I don't want to crush my sombrero.' She struggled to sit herself upright.

'Then slip it off your shoulder, until it's time to put it on for your act.'

Tyler reached and unbuttoned the tab on the shoulder of Cara's bolero that held the chin strap of the sombrero for carrying purposes. The touch of his fingers scorched through the soft velvet of the jacket, and she caught a sharp breath as he released the hat, and rested it in front of her across her knees, holding it there with his slim, tanned fingers on the brim.

'Here comes Ben.' He directed her attention to the floor.

The clown tumbled into the room, tripping over his outsized boots, and making the children laugh, but Cara hardly noticed him. Her eyes gazed unseeingly at Ben's antics with the dogs, while her mind's eye registered every minute detail of Tyler, sitting behind her.

Thank goodness she had pushed the pen into the sack of presents, and not put it back into her pocket, she thought. If the hard edge of the presentation case had dug into Tyler as she lay against him, he might have removed that too, and discovered that it was meant for him.

Her narrow escape brought a warm tide of colour rushing to her cheeks, and Tyler's mouth murmured in her ear, 'Are you too hot?' Proving that he had not been watching the clown, either.

The discovery warmed her cheeks to a deeper hue, and she answered breathlessly, 'No, I'm fine.' And wished she had said, 'Yes,' so that he would have released her to sit by herself. And immediately felt glad that he had not.

Her mind told her to do one thing, while her heart told her to do just the opposite, and she felt like a Christmas cracker, being pulled apart between the two.

Determinedly she fixed her eyes on the clown. By this time Ben had several of the children from the audience out in the front, helping him, encouraged by Mario and another of the older children from the circus.

'Ben's good with children, isn't he?' Tyler said in her ear.

'He loves them. Which is just as well, as he'll soon have two of his own. You can't be averse to them yourself, to invite this crowd into your home,' Cara retorted feelingly as a roar of laughter at the clown's antics nearly split the roof.

The tip of her ear tingled to Tyler's voice, and instinctively she tried to raise her hand to rub it, but Tyler's arms round her trapped her own to her sides, and she dropped her hand helplessly back on to her lap.

He would be wonderful with children. And it was inviting self-destruction to allow her mind to project into the future, and visualise him with his own children. And Rosemary's.

Cara dared not allow herself to dwell on it now. Desperately she begged him, 'Let me go. It's time I got ready for my act. I've got things to do.'

'What things?' You're already dressed in your costume, and Mario's only just begun his juggling act. The magician comes next.'

'Those two acts don't take long. Please, Tyler.'

Cara did not specify what things she had to do, but the urgency in her voice must have convinced him, because he opened his arms and released her, and she slid off the window-seat and felt cold and forsaken, standing on her own.

Her mind was in a whirl, and the only thing she had to do was to try to calm it before she began her act.

She hurried away to the entrance hall, collapsing on to a settle beside the waiting Pepi, and thanked her lucky stars that the magician spoke so little English, which effectively deterred him from attempting a conversation with her.

Pepi's turn came, and gave Cara a few merciful minutes on her own in which to try to compose herself, before it was her turn to perform. What had Tyler called the lasso-dancing? Clever. Fascinating. Cara dropped her head on to her hands, and willed herself to relax.

Loud applause brought her upright again, and she heard one of the teachers announce brightly, 'Now Cara will dance for you with a lasso. Watch carefully, and see if you can remember how to do it for yourself, when you go home.'

Cara's eyes searched the audience, but the green-eyed girl of the screen was not among them. They flew to the window-seat, and she was not there either, and Cara despised herself for the relief that flooded through her because the place beside Tyler was still empty.

The rope became a live thing in her hands. Her young audience ceased to exist, and she was aware only of Tyler, watching her from deep in the shadows of the window-seat. This was the last time she would perform in front of him, and it had to be perfect.

The lasso circled and spun, whirling round her dancing feet, her slender, gyrating body, and up over her head into the air and back again, while her heels tapped an inspired rhythm on the parquet floor.

A thought strayed across Cara's mind. When Rosemary returned, would Tyler sit in the window-seat with her?

The rope wavered and went slack, and Cara gave it a desperate twist of her wrist to regain control, and danced on, tortured by what could be the only possible answer to her question.

'That was smashing, miss. Will you show me how to do it?' A small, freckled-faced boy in the audience called out to her as the clapping died away, and Cara forced a smile to her face.

'After tea,' she promised, and joined Mario and Pepi on the front row of chairs. She did not attempt to return to the window. Her only hope of retaining her self-control lay in staying as far away from Tyler as possible.

'Before we have our tea, shall we say a special thank-you to Cara, for helping to entertain us today?'

Her ploy was unsuccessful. Tyler rose to his feet and strolled towards her, and Cara's breath stilled. In his hand he held a parcel. It must have been behind him on the window-seat all the time, and she had not noticed.

'Thank you, Cara.'

Amid a burst of clapping, Tyler gave the box into her hands. His eyes raked her face, and she dropped her own confusedly to see what the box contained.

It was cellophane-covered, with a red-ribbon bow, and, she saw with catching breath, it was filled with beautiful hothouse flowers. Vivid primulas gazed back at her, and gentle pansy faces. Bright-eyed daisies nestled in soft moss beside nosegays of violets entwined among tiny, trailing ivy leaves.

Rosemary had worn an orchid.

Cara stammered her thanks, forcing the words out from lips that felt stiff. She pinned the smile on her face, while her heart broke at the beauty of Tyler's flowers, mourning because they were the impersonal gift of a kindly host to a performer at his children's party, and not a living, loving message from him, especially for her.

Cara hugged the box of flowers to her as the headmistress called out, 'Now, children, take your chairs, and go and sit round the tea-table. The big ones help the little ones. Quietly, now.'

Chairs scraped, and confusion reigned, washing round herself and Tyler, parting them as the children broke ranks and headed towards the laden trestle table at the far end of the room.

Over the heads of the children, Tyler's eyes sought

Cara's face, his look enigmatic, but two small girls, energetically pulling their chairs backwards towards the tea-table, collided with his legs, and tumbled over, helplessly entangling themselves with their burdens, and claiming his attention.

Tyler bent to extricate the children, and Cara escaped into the general mêlée round the tea-table, first putting her flowers carefully on the safety of the window-seat. They would fade, as eventually the pain of her love must fade, or she could not continue to live. But each year, when spring brought its new blooms, it would remind her.

'Where are you going to sit, Cara?' Ben called over to her.

'I'll sit here.'

It was the side of the table farthest away from where Tyler stood, and among a group of boisterous juniors, which included the freckle-faced boy who wanted to learn lasso-dancing, and it gave Cara the perfect excuse to concentrate on the children instead of their host.

'You sit on the other side, Mario,' Ben told the young juggler. 'Your father and I will take each end of the table.'

The clown ambled off to his seat among the little ones, taking the dogs with him, carrying out the promise that the performers would share themselves out among the children sitting at the table.

As a distraction, her own table companions could not be bettered. They fired an endless stream of questions at Cara. How did she handle the rope? Did lasso-dancing take long to learn? And she was kept so busy answering them that she was not aware of Tyler standing behind her until he asked,

'Would you like some jelly?'

She spun round, startled. She had forgotten Daniels saying Tyler intended to help serve his young guests himself. Tyler's eyes mocked her as he stood with a bowl of bright red jelly poised in his one hand, a large spoonful of its contents held aloft, awaiting her choice.

I prefer jelly ... His eyes laughed at her, silently repeating his taunt, and Cara stiffened.

'You eat it.' She eyed the wobbly spoonful with a baleful look. 'You said you preferred jelly.'

Deliberately she turned to face the table again, presenting her back stiffly towards him.

'I'm strongly tempted to tip it down your stubborn little neck.'

Instead of moving on with his burden, and offering it to someone else, as she expected him to, he moved closer in behind her, leaning forward to speak into her ear, and pressing against the back of her chair, pushing her remorselessly up against the edge of the table. Cara gasped.

'On second thoughts, it would be a wicked waste of good jelly,' he said at last, and moved on, handing out liberal helpings to her eager table companions.

Cara went limp. Her appetite for the goodies on the table vanished. She was trembling, and to cover it she reached for her cup of tea, and picked up the spoon.

It clattered like a castanet against the saucer, and she put it down again hurriedly, but not before Tyler had heard it. He was bending to serve jelly to one of his young guests on the opposite side of the table, and at the hard, sharp clink of metal against china, his eyes lanced across the white cloth, and fixed themselves on Cara's face.

His look was sardonic, arrogant in the certainty of his power to make her tremble, and her eyes meeting his hated him for his arrogance, and his power over her. And she knew, as he did, that she was helpless against both.

'Who's ready for Christmas cake?' Mrs Turner called out brightly.

Cara felt ready to weep. But not now. Not here. Later, when she could escape from the party, and shut herself into the privacy of her living-van, on her own.

'Who's going to blow out the candles on the cake for me, before I start to cut it?' Mrs Turner wanted to know. 'Mr Tyler?'

'Yes, I'll blow them out for you.'

Obligingly Tyler put down the empty jelly-bowl and

rounded the table in three long strides, and announced, 'Cara will help me.'

'Why choose me? Why not one of the children?' Cara stammered, taken aback by his unexpected move.

'I'm sure you'll do it beautifully.'

Every eye in the room was watching her. Tyler's hands came down to rest on her shoulders, urging her to her feet. Making it impossible for her to refuse. Cara rose and walked jerkily beside him to the top of the table.

'Blow when I do,' he said. 'If you blow out the candles, you get a wish.'

'I thought you only wished on a birthday cake?'

You could wish on wedding cake, too, but only on someone else's wedding cake. The urge to weep became stronger, almost more than Cara could control.

'You can wish on a Christmas cake, too, if it's a special one,' Tyler was saying. 'This one is special, isn't it, children?'

'Yes,' they chorused back, and Tyler drew her close to his side. 'Take a deep breath . . .'

With his arm round her, supporting her against him, Cara found it difficult to breathe properly at all. She stood tensely at his side, conscious of the sea of eyes watching her, desperately conscious of the hard, muscular leanness of Tyler pressing her to him.

'Count three, and then blow with me,' he instructed her.

He did not need her help. He could easily have managed to blow out the small ring of candles in the middle of the huge iced cake. And if she succeeded in blowing them out first time, Cara thought bleakly, it was of no use her making a wish. What her heart wished for could not possibly come true.

What would Tyler wish for, if he wished at all?

Rosemary? Again, her question answered itself.

And Tyler's wish would come true.

CHAPTER TEN

THEY blew together, and the ring of candles in the centre of the cake flickered and died. Thin spirals of smoke rose from the blackened wicks, and a blackness descended upon Cara's spirits to match.

She felt as if her heart had been extinguished, along with the candles.

In spite of the light from the glittering chandeliers overhead, the room seemed to go dark round her. A tiny silence of anti-climax descended on the party, and then a buzz of noise arose again as the housekeeper began to wield her knife on the iced masterpiece.

'Will you have your piece of cake here, Miss Varelli?' Mrs Turner invited.

Cara shook her head. 'I don't want any cake,' she refused.

'Wrap up a piece for her, Mrs Turner. She can eat it later on.'

Even in such a small matter as a piece of cake, Tyler had his way. Cara stood in mutinous silence as the housekeeper wrapped a slice of cake in a paper napkin and tucked it into the pocket of her bolero, and Tyler said,

'If you've finished your tea, come and sit on the window-seat, out of the way of the scrum.'

'I'll go and tidy myself up first. I feel a wreck,' Cara refused hastily, and while Mrs Turner gave Tyler a plate of cake to distribute to the children, distracting his attention, she slipped away from under his arm.

She gained the cloakroom and subsided on to a stool in front of one of the big mirrors. Her eyes looked back at her from the glass, huge, dark, and bright with unshed tears, and with an exclamation of impatience she slipped off her bolero and bathed her face in warm, scented water.

The piece of wrapped cake protruded temptingly

170

from her pocket, but she left it where it was. She would give it to Poppy when she returned to the circus, as a small thank-you for the loan of her costume.

She was patting her face dry with a soft towel, spinning out the time away from the ballroom for as long as possible, when a small girl popped her head round the door and said shyly, 'The boys sent me to say you promised to teach them how to do lasso-dancing, after tea.'

'I'm just coming,' Cara smiled back.

Little boys did not worry her. It was their grown-up counterpart who was capable of turning her world upside down, and the one would prove an ideal refuge from the other. She followed the child back into the ballroom, and was instantly surrounded by eager would-be lasso-dancers.

This gave her the perfect excuse, when Tyler came up and asked her, 'Would you like to come and try your hand at the coconut-shy with me?' to answer blithely, as if she had not got a care in the world, 'You go. I've got too many pupils to cope with here.'

And she swung her lasso, and danced to delight the children, while her heart disintegrated inside her.

'Listen, everybody. I thought I heard sleigh bells.'

With a motherly instinct for timing that took the increasingly boisterous games of tag as a signal that the novelty of the fairground booths was at last diminishing, the housekeeper's upraised hand brought instant silence to the room.

'It must be Father Christmas. Come and sit down round the Christmas tree quickly. The little ones at the front, the taller ones behind.' The teachers took up the cue, and Cara's pupils vanished in favour of the new attraction.

Tyler disappeared too, no doubt to the ante-room to change into his scarlet robes and pick up his sack of presents. A quiver of anticipation ran through Cara. Soon, he would find his own present at the bottom of the sack.

He would wonder who it had come from. Nerves curled in the pit of Cara's stomach in case he should ask questions as to who the donor might be. But he could not discover who had sent him the pen unless she herself told him, because nobody else knew of its existence.

The knowledge unknotted her stomach, and she wriggled back into the shadows of the window embrasure to watch the proceedings, confident that her secret was safe.

'A happy Christmas, children,' the red-robed figure called out gruffly.

Tyler made an impressive Santa Claus. His robes accentuated his height, and the long, snowy beard did nothing to diminish the sweetness of his smile as the children roared their welcome.

'Let me see what I've got in here.' He set the sack of presents down on the floor, and an expectant hush descended upon the assembly as he reached in an exploring hand. 'Clive Roberts.' He read the label clearly. 'Which one is Clive?'

A small boy hurried up to receive his present, and thanked Tyler for it shyly, and a little girl followed next, and as Tyler bent down to give her her gift, she flung chubby arms round his neck and kissed him soundly before running back to her place, hugging her parcel.

The boys were more reticent, but the other small girls all followed suit, and a lump rose unbidden in Cara's throat as she watched their innocent pleasure, caught up in spite of herself by the magic of Christmas. By the magic of Tyler, who was uninhibitedly enjoying himself in his new role.

'Cara Varelli,' he called. 'Where's Cara got to?'

Cara was so absorbed in watching him, that Tyler called her name twice before she realised it was her own.

'Here she is, Santa. Come through this way, Miss Varelli.'

Cara stumbled to her feet, startled, as hands reached in and drew her from the friendly shadows of the window recess, and a teacher made a path for her through the seated children.

Tyler waited for her at the other end. 'A happy Christmas, Cara.'

He gave her the same greeting that he gave to the children, but the look in his eyes was very different from the avuncular gaze he bent upon his small guests. It set Cara's pulses racing madly as he pressed a small, gift-wrapped box into her nerveless fingers.

'Th ... thank you,' she managed to stammer.

'Thank you? Is that all?'

White cotton-wool eyebrows rose, and twin devils of mischief danced below them, in tawny eyes that, because he was Santa Claus, ought to have been blue, Cara thought bemusedly.

'What do you mean?' Her wildly beating heart knew very well what he meant, as she knew that he did not intend to allow her to escape.

'All the other young ladies kissed me, when they said thank you,' he reproached her gravely.

'I ... you ...'

Cara longed to smack him. She longed to run. But her parcel occupied her hands, and her feet seemed unaccountably to be rooted to the floor. An encouraging cheer rose from the children, and before she could step out of his reach Santa Claus bent his head above her, and claimed her lips with his own.

'Happy Christmas, Cara,' his deep voice said.

His eyes glowed like molten fire from the depths of his cotton-wool disguise. The beard tickled her cheeks and her chin, and even if she had not been aware of who it was beneath the scarlet robes, there was no disguising the identity of the lips that took masterful possession of her shrinking mouth.

She stumbled back to her seat in the window to the accompaniment of clapping from the children. Behind her, Tyler continued to call out names and hand out presents from the sack. She heard the teacher say, 'What did Father Christmas bring you, Miss Varelli?' and began obediently to open her parcel.

She had not expected to be included among the recipients. Tyler had already given her flowers, and now this. She caught her breath as she lifted the tiny silver panda brooch from its deep bed of velvet. It was the symbol of the World Wildlife Fund which was to be the beneficiary from the film she had seen in London, a delightful souvenir of the day she had spent in London with Tyler.

It would remind her most of all of Rosemary.

'Do pin it on your bolero,' the teacher urged her admiringly. 'It'll show up beautifully against the black velvet.'

Cara fixed it with fingers that shook. The silver winked against the soft black velvet, catching the light from the chandeliers. She caught Tyler's eye. He looked across at her, and smiled, a satisfied smile, and she felt a quick stab of resentment that even at a distance he was able to manipulate her to do just what he wanted.

She watched him tensely as he delved ever deeper into the sack of presents. Surely soon he must come to his own? He brought it out, the very last present, and Cara held her breath.

'Is there anyone who hasn't had a present yet?' he enquired in a puzzled voice. 'There seems to be one left over.'

He thumbed open the gift tag, and Cara's fingers gripped tightly together, going white with the pressure she put on them, but she was unaware of the pain. Only aware that Tyler was holding her present to him.

'To Father Christmas, with love,' he read aloud in a surprised voice. 'But the label doesn't say who it's from,' he added, and looked straight across at Cara.

He knew.

The shock of it stopped the breath in Cara's throat. Tyler's eyes seemed to bore right into her, burning a hole through her mind. He had guessed. But how? Her numbed brain refused the conundrum, but his look told her he knew he had guessed correctly.

He must not thank her for the pen. Not in front of all these people. If he did, it would betray her secret, and make her humiliation complete. Cara's eyes beseeched him, begging him for this one mercy.

It was bad enough that Tyler had discovered her secret. But if he thanked her for the pen, and made the knowledge public . . . She felt the blood drain from her face, leaving it as white as her twisting fingers.

'Let's all join hands and sing a carol before we go. Don't forget to collect your balloons from Ben the clown, as you go to fetch your coats,' Tyler urged.

'Away in a manger . . .' He raised his voice and led the singing.

He had not betrayed her. Her secret was safe, from the others, if not from him. Slowly Cara unlocked her fingers, and drew in a long, shuddering breath.

'No crib for a bed . . .'

Tyler led the singing in a rich, strong baritone, and Cara drank in the sound of his voice, absorbing it with the thirst of a sponge for water.

The scene would remain in her memory for as long as she lived. The lighted Christmas tree. The upturned faces of the lustily singing children. And Tyler, shouldering the yoke of his inheritance, fitting into it with an ease and dignity that proclaimed it as his own. A lump stopped her aching throat, preventing her from joining in the singing.

Rosemary would fit into the scene with the same effortless ease. Next year she would stand beside him, helping him to lead the singing.

'Come and get your balloons, children. One each,' the teacher called.

The carol came to an end, and Ben began to distribute the balloons. A big red balloon burst, and the well-trained dogs ducked their heads under their paws, pretending to stop their ears, and causing a burst of merriment among the departing children.

The headmistress turned to speak to Tyler, and he waited courteously to hear her out. She held out her hand, evidently thanking him for the party, and he smiled, and then she turned away to follow the children out of the room.

Tyler turned, too, and began to walk towards Cara.

His stride was swift, and purposeful, and his long red cloak billowed out behind him with the speed of his steps as he came towards her. Cara gripped the edge of the window-seat with nervous fingers, and her tongue

flicked across suddenly parched lips as he came to a
halt in front of her, and growled through his cotton-
wool beard,

'It's time you and I had a talk.'

'We've got nothing to t-talk about,' she stammered,
her heart beginning to thump.

The only thing Tyler could want to talk about was
the pen, and it was the very last thing she wanted to
discuss.

She squirmed inwardly as she remembered the words
she had written on the gift card. What had possessed
her to bare her heart in writing like that, and risk his
guessing its source?

How had he guessed?

'We've got plenty,' he retorted. 'To start with, I think
a few explanations are in order.'

'B-but . . .'

'Come into my study. It's quieter there, and I can get
out of this rig-out. It's confoundedly hot.'

Cara felt icy cold. She gave a hunted look round the
room, but the only way out was blocked by children
and teachers filing through the door, and there was no
escape that way.

Tyler reached down determined hands, and lifted her
to her feet, and keeping hold of her he steered her with
him towards the door.

'That's the last balloon gone. Come on, dogs, it's
time to go home.' Ben grinned at them cheerfully as
they reached the door together.

'Stay on for a while, Ben. We're all going to sit down
and have a quiet drink together, to get our breaths
back,' Tyler invited, and the clown's grin broadened.

'That sounds like a wonderful idea. I'll go and explain
to Pepi.' He hurried away, the pack of terriers trotting at
his heels, and Tyler placed a steel arm across Cara's
shoulders and turned her towards the study door.

'My lord? Oh, there you are.' The housekeeper
hurried across from the front door. 'Miss Rosemary's
just arrived. Her taxi's at the bottom of the steps now.'

Tyler's hand slackened its grip on Cara's shoulder,
and his arm lifted away from her.

'Rosemary?' His eyes lit up. He pushed back the scarlet hood from off his head, and with a swift tug removed cotton-wool eyebrows, moustache and beard from his face. The girl Cara had last seen on film appeared in the doorway.

'Tyler . . . darling!'

He held out wide arms, and she ran straight into them, like a bird reaching its nest after a long flight.

Cara caught a flash of bronze. Bronze travelling-suit, expensively tailored. Necklace and earrings to match, setting off a high-necked cream cashmere sweater. Green eyes, clear, wide, and even lovelier than they had appeared on the screen.

Her own had probably turned the same feline shade, Cara decided bitterly. The girl was taller than she was herself, but not so tall as Tyler. Queenly. They made a handsome couple.

Numbly Cara started to walk. Not to the study. Tyler would not want to talk to her, now that Rosemary had come. Her feet carried her past the study door without a glance, and straight on through the open double doors through which the girl had just come.

A man was bending over an accumulation of luggage stacked outside, and she passed him by without speaking, and walked on, down the stone steps, on to the gravel drive, away from the lights of the house towards the silent Park. The night would receive her, and in the merciful darkness she could let the tears flow.

She felt very tired.

The unmistakable rattle of a diesel engine sounded on the Park drive behind her. The taxi was returning to the village. The driver must have carried all the luggage into the hall.

Hardly aware of her own actions, Cara stood four-square in the glare of the oncoming headlights, and raised her hand to signal the vehicle to stop. Obediently it pulled to a halt beside her, and the passenger door opened in a yawning black chasm.

She got in. 'The entrance to the circus, please.' She slammed the door behind her and turned in her seat as the cab started off, and a bulk of darkness moved in the far corner.

'Who . . .?' Cara's voice choked into stunned silence. She blinked to adjust her eyes to the near darkness, and her heart hammered with suffocating force. She could not possibly mistake the sharp planes of the face etched against the far window of the cab. 'What are you doing here?' she gasped.

'I told you it was time we had a talk. Since you didn't condescend to wait for me in the library, we'll go to your van and talk there,' Tyler told her curtly.

'I said we'd got nothing to talk about. And anyway, why should I wait for you?'

Cara rounded on him, stung out of her trance by his arrogant assumption that she would be willing to wait meekly in the library until he chose to come to her. Straight from Rosemary's arms. The memory was like a spear shafting through her.

'You were otherwise engaged,' she spat angrily. 'Rosemary . . .'

'Taxi-drivers aren't deaf,' he reminded her sharply, and she drew in a hissing breath and subsided into her seat.

The journey to the circus was only of a few minutes' duration, but to Cara it seemed to last for ever. The silence was charged with a thousand electric sparks, exploding like meteorites as they met and clashed in the darkness between them.

Anger, and defiance. She could feel Tyler's anger, like a dark stormcloud reaching out to engulf her, and her mind wrestled with questions which she dared not ask.

Why had he left Rosemary, to follow her?

Had her blatant message on the gift-tag decided him to come after her, and tell her bluntly that she was not for him? That now Rosemary was here, he did not want to see her again?

Her heart twisted with anguish. She crouched in the corner of the cab, and made no attempt to disembark when it drew up at the circus entrance.

'Are you going to get out, or do I have to carry you?' Tyler asked silkily when she did not move, and the menace in his voice warned Cara that in spite of the presence of the taxi-driver he would carry out his threat unless she joined him of her own accord.

Reluctantly she forced her trembling legs to step out of the cab door, which Tyler held wide open for her.

'Wait for me,' he instructed the driver, and taking Cara by the arm before she could dodge round him, he marched her in the direction of her van.

'I don't want to talk with you,' she gritted. 'I've got nothing to say.'

'Good,' Tyler interjected curtly. 'In that case, I'll do the talking, and you can listen to me.'

'I won't let you into my van.'

'In my limited experience of circus life, the van doors are never locked.'

He marched Cara up the van steps, and she felt like a prisoner mounting the scaffold. Tyler deposited her ungently into the chair in front of her dressing-table, and leaning back against the edge of the bed opposite he loomed over her, and demanded,

'Now perhaps you'll be good enough to explain why you walked out on me and my guests.'

His face was set and hard, and white under its surface tan, pale with the force of the anger that consumed him. It was vibrant in his voice, in the paleness of his tensed knuckles.

'I wasn't obliged to stay on,' Cara defended herself spiritedly. 'My contract was to entertain the children, and the children have gone.'

'You heard me tell Ben that we were all going to sit down together for a quiet drink and a breather before we split up.'

'Oh yes, I heard you *tell* Ben,' Cara flared. 'But I'm not so inclined as Ben to do as I'm told. If you want people to stay for a drink, it's usual to invite them, not tell them.'

'It *was* an invitation.'

'Which Ben accepted. And I refused.'

'Were you in such a hurry to get back to the circus that half an hour would have made all that much difference?' Tyler asked her angrily. 'That you were prepared to walk back alone across the Park, rather than wait, and go with the others in the van?'

'I wanted a breath of fresh air. I—I'd got a headache.'

It was her heart that ached, not her head, and no amount of fresh air could cure that.

'Was your headache so bad that you couldn't wait for a few more minutes to be introduced to my sister and her fiancé?'

'Your ... sister?' Cara blurted, and stared at him, stunned.

'As soon as I'd said hello to Rosemary, I turned round to introduce you, and you'd gone, without even saying good night. John was sorting out their luggage on the steps, ready to bring it into the house, and he said you'd walked past him in the direction of the Park. I made the excuse to them that you'd probably gone back to your van to change. But now I want to know the real reason,' he demanded harshly.

'Rosemary's your *sister*?'

Cara hardly heard the rest of what he said. Only one thing registered on her dazed mind, and she did not know whether to believe it, or to pinch herself to see if she were dreaming.

'Of course she's my sister. What do you keep on about Rosemary for?' Tyler demanded impatiently. 'You read the article in *Personalities*. You must know our entire life history from that. If you want all the i's dotted, and the t's crossed, she's actually my half-sister. I don't think the magazine reporter got round to that bit.' There was a thin edge of sarcasm to his voice. 'My father married again after my mother died, and Ros came along when I was about eight. She was an engaging little brat.' His lips tilted upwards in the same soft smile he had given to Rosemary's screen image. 'It was nice to have another child in the family, but it explains why we're not much alike to look at. But all this is beside the point.'

It was the only point that mattered, to Cara. 'I didn't read the article in *Personalities*, I only saw the picture,' she confessed in a small voice.

'You didn't . . . but you said . . .'

Tyler's eyes bored into her own, measuring the implications of what she had just told him.

'I didn't see the whole magazine. Linda only gave me the front cover.'

'Linda? The little . . .' Enlightenment and fury fought for supremacy on Tyler's rock-hard face. 'It's a good job for Linda she's left the circus,' he ground out at last.

'How do you know she's gone?' Cara asked faintly. Her mind spun. Everything was happening too quickly for her to be able to grasp.

'I can use my eyes. There are two gaps in the line of vans, where Gio and Linda were parked.'

So much for her earlier excuse that Linda was indisposed. Cara twisted her fingers together in her lap, her eyes downcast.

'If you didn't know Rosemary was my sister, who did you think she was?'

'I . . .' The words stuck in Cara's throat. How to answer such a question?

'Tell me.' Tyler reached out and drew Cara into his arms, and her eyes flew up, startled, to his face. 'Did you think she was a girlfriend?' he insisted, and watched the warm tide of colour rise across her throat and cheeks, answering for her.

'It wasn't any of my business.' Cara grasped ineffectually at her shreds of pride. 'You and I . . . we weren't . . . we aren't . . .' She could not go on.

'*I* was. And *I* am,' Tyler said, his voice low. 'What about you, Cara? Did you mean the message you wrote on your card? Don't try to deny you wrote it. I recognised your writing, from the day you came to the Hall to take down details of the party.'

His fingers held her chin, so that she could not look away. Her heart fluttered like a trapped bird in her breast. Surely he must feel the frantic beat of it against his chest, so closely did he strain her to him.

'Do you remember what it was you wrote?' he insisted, when she did not answer, and when she nodded dumbly, 'Tell me,' he commanded.

'To—to Father Christmas. With—with love.'

Oh, he was cruel, to humiliate her so. Cara's eyes sparkled with threatened tears.

'Did you mean it, Cara? With love?' Suddenly his hand left her chin and joined his other arm round her, crushing her to him. 'Oh, my heart. My darling. Tell me you meant it,' he groaned. 'It'll destroy me, if you didn't. Oh Cara, Cara, I love you.'

It could not be true. It could not be happening. She *must* be dreaming.

But Tyler's arms were real, straining her to him. His lips were real, as they burned his passion in indelible kisses on her mouth, her cheeks, her throat. 'I love you. I love you,' he muttered hoarsely.

His head lifted, and his eyes burned into Cara's in an agony of entreaty. 'Tell me you meant your message. Tell me that you love me,' he begged her brokenly.

'I love you.'

The words came out on a long-drawn sigh, and Tyler's eyes fired, burning like molten gold as they searched her face.

'Say it again,' he begged, with the thirst of a man who could never hear it repeated often enough.

'I love you.' Cara's arms rose and twined themselves round his neck, drawing his head down closer to reach her lips, while her fingers twined their ecstasy in the crisp, tawny mane of his hair.

An eternity of time passed, and then . . .

'When?' Cara whispered.

'I knew the first moment I set eyes on you, in the Park. You looked a vision on your spotted horse. And then, when I saw your paper flowers, I wanted to give you real ones.'

'You shouted at me for belonging to the circus,' Cara remembered, running her fingers along the crisp, waving line of his hair.

'I was a brute. A beast. I'll make it up to you, I promise.' His lips begged her forgiveness.

'I thought you were just playing with me.'

'Never. I told you that day on the beach I wasn't playing, and I meant it. When you intend to spend the rest of your life with someone, it's too serious a thing for play. Play is for children. Marriage is for adults.'

He cradled her in his arms as if he never intended to let her go.

'Is that what you wanted to talk to me about, in the library?' Cara wanted to know mischievously.

'Witch!' He kissed away the demure look in her eyes, and brought them back to sparkling life. 'I wanted to know how soon you'd marry me.'

'You haven't asked me if I will, yet,' she teased.

'Don't torment me.' The laughter fled, and Tyler buried his face in the darkness of her hair, and the agony in his voice made her instantly relent.

'As soon as you like,' she whispered, so low that her voice was no more than a summer breeze, but Tyler heard it, and his head lifted with an ardent look that brought shy colour flooding to her cheeks.

'Now isn't soon enough. I can't bear to be away from you.' He traced her tremulous smile with his lips. 'I love you so much. I shan't be happy until you're mine. I've been tormented by the thought that you and Gio . . .'

'Gio?' Cara exclaimed in astonishment. 'But you heard me tell Mrs Wallace I didn't intend to marry Gio.'

'I thought you were just trying to silence her tactless tongue. And then I saw you with Gio in front of the jeweller's window in Broadwater, and I looked at your hand each time I saw you in case you wore a ring.'

'I wanted a brooch for Aunt Beth for Christmas. I got a silver and coral one. I'll show you.'

'Not now. Later.' He occupied the time with more important things than coral brooches, and when at last he freed her mouth, and she leaned back, flushed and bright-eyed against his shoulder, he confessed: 'I couldn't be sure about you and Gio, even though you didn't wear a ring. Even when he got drunk, you defended him. And in the car, coming back from London, you said you didn't hate him. Women are funny that way.'

'I don't think I'm capable of hating anyone. Only of loving.'

'And of being loved. Oh Cara, darling, I adore you.'
He imprinted his vow on her lips, and promised, 'If we
get wanderlust, we'll go on safari together, but there'll
always be home to come back to. The Hall will be the
first settled home either of us has ever known.' His eyes
glowed at the prospect of sharing it with her.

'Rosemary will be thinking you've abandoned the
Hall for good, by now.'

'Heavens, I'd forgotten Rosemary and John.
Although I don't expect they'll mind. They're planning
their own honeymoon. I suggested they combined it
with the team's next safari in the summer,' Tyler
grinned.

'Is that what you want, for us?'

'Certainly not. I don't intend to share you with
anyone on our honeymoon. I don't want any
distractions. Only you,' he assured her with satisfying
conviction. 'There's one small formality first, though.'
He drew her to her feet. 'Let's go and get Mitch's
blessing, and your aunt's.'

They entered the older couple's van, and Tyler
smiled. 'I don't think we need to tell them our news.
They look as if they might have guessed already,' he
said as two expectant faces turned towards them.

'Here's to your future.' Mitcham Brook laughed at
their surprise as he produced a bottle and four glasses.

'Champagne?' Cara gasped. 'Where did you get this
from?'

'I've been keeping it for a special occasion,' her uncle
said mysteriously, and relented with a laugh, 'They say
lookers-on see most of the game. Bless you both.' He
raised his glass in a heartfelt toast.

'Come back with us to the Hall afterwards,' Tyler
invited the pair when the excitement of congratulations
had died down a little. 'We'll collect Poppy, too, it will
be a pleasant break for her now the noise of the party is
over.'

'Before we go, I've got some news to tell you as well,'
Mitcham Brook observed, and smiled at their interested
looks. 'Ben's agreed to become my partner.'

Beth twinkled. 'Mitch has got his eye firmly on the

future. Ben will eventually have two partners to carry on from him, when his sons grow up.'

'How do you know they'll be sons?' Cara felt bewildered at the speed at which everything was happening at once.

'Poppy says she's certain they're both boys,' her aunt chuckled, 'and she's the one who should know.'

'I'm so glad, Uncle Mitch.' Cara reached out and grasped his gnarled hand. 'You and Aunt Beth ought to be taking things more quietly now. Sharing the load a bit. When I go, there'll be three short in the troupe, now you've lost Gio and Linda as well,' she realised remorsefully.

'Not for long, my dear,' the circus-owner said reassuringly. 'The Fazels have agreed to join us.'

'The Fazels? What stupendous luck,' Cara exclaimed, and turned to explain to Tyler, 'They're the very cream of trapeze artists.'

'Even better, they're bringing Wyn Fazel's younger sister with them. She's a versatile artist. She's already a juggler and an acrobat, and she's learning the trapeze to stand in for her sister when necessary.'

'Everything seems to be coming right all at once,' Cara smiled happily.

'With Ben sharing the management of the circus, that means you and Beth will be able to take a break now and then,' Tyler put in thoughtfully.

'We'd thought about it, in a year or two's time,' Beth confessed.

'Why not break yourselves in gently, and use the Lodge at the end of the Park road as your over-wintering home for a while, and consider making it your permanent home when you want to give up travelling altogether?' Tyler suggested gravely. 'It's a cosy little cottage, just right for two, and there's an acre or two of paddock attached to it, where you could raise your miniatures.'

Tyler smiled at the looks of incredulous delight that spread across the two older faces confronting him, and went on, 'It would be nice for Cara and me to have you both close to us, and if the circus over-wintered at

Broadwater each year, you wouldn't be entirely cut off from your old life. I've had a letter from the local authority this morning, giving me planning permission to landscape the lower field, and turn it into a permanent over-wintering site for the circus, if you agree. There'll be hard standing for the vans, and all mains services laid on. No more walking across a muddy field for Ben to attend to the generator,' he joked.

'If you had the letter this morning, that means you must have applied for planning permission before you knew I'd marry you,' Cara accused him, when the older couple had gone to collect their coats.

'I had to make sure the circus would return to the Park each year, and bring you with it,' Tyler told her soberly, and she stilled, caught by the deep tremor of emotion in his voice. 'Even if you had chosen to marry someone from the circus world, I had to make sure you would come back to the Park again each winter, so that at least I'd be able to see you and speak to you again. I couldn't bear the thought of losing you entirely. That's why I kept your plastic pen that you lent me in the store, because it was something that belonged to you.'

His voice broke, and it was a minute or two before he was able to continue, 'It had to be you, or no one, for me,' he told her huskily.

'*You* are my world. Now, and for always.' Cara wound her arms round him, and kissed back the glow to his eyes and the laughter to his lips.

'In that case, you'd better wear this, to let the rest of the world know,' Tyler teased.

He delved into his pocket and brought out an exquisitely enamelled ring-case, lined with soft velvet, and Cara gasped her delight. 'It's beautiful.'

'Let me see if it fits.' Gently he lifted her left hand and slid the glittering sapphire and diamond ring on to her third finger. 'Hmm, not bad.' He folded her close, and his voice was husky against her mouth as he said,

'It'll look even better when you're wearing a wedding ring to go with it.'

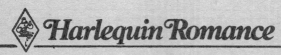
Harlequin Romance

Coming Next Month

2815 DRAGON SEA Bethany Campbell
Dragon Sea, the deserted stone mansion she loves, should have
been hers. So how can this young Maine woman accept the
new owner—the very man who destroyed her dreams once
already?

2816 WALK INTO TOMORROW Rosemary Carter
A teahouse proprietor in the Canadian Rockies needs to get
over the trauma of the past before thinking about the future.
But the persistently friendly owner of a local hotel won't wait!

2817 PLAIN JANE Rosemary Hammond
Seattle's most eligible male hires a garden editor to landscape
his new home, and then pursues her. Irresistible men don't
pursue plain-Janes with any serious intentions, do they?

2818 THE GLASS MADONNA Liza Manning
The respected master of dei Santi Glassworks expects an older,
more mature student to train with his traditional craftsmen—
someone who's come to Italy to learn about Venetian glass, not
love. What he gets is Miranda....

2819 WILD FOR TO HOLD Annabel Murray
Hard times force a determined tomboy and her grandmother to
sell their Lake District farm. But when the new owner tries to
control more than the land, he has a fight on his hands.

2820 INNOCENT IN EDEN Margaret Way
An assistant scriptwriter discovers scandal in an Australian
family's past...and a fiery, consuming love that's very much in
the present.

Available in February wherever paperback books are sold,
or through Harlequin Reader Service.

In the U.S.
P.O. Box 1397
Buffalo, N.Y.
14240-1397

In Canada
P.O. Box 603
Fort Erie, Ontario
L2A 5X3

Here's how to get this special offer from Harlequin!
As simple as 1...2...3!

January
BETTY NEELS
TREASURY EDITION
COUPON

1. **Each month, save one Treasury Edition coupon from your favorite Romance or Presents novel.**
2. **In four months you'll have saved four Treasury Edition coupons (only one coupon per month allowed).**
3. **Then all you have to do is fill out and return the order form provided, along with the four Treasury Edition coupons required and $2.95 for postage and handling.**

Mail to: Harlequin Reader Service

In the U.S.A.	In Canada
901 Fuhrmann Blvd.	P.O. Box 609
P.O. Box 1397	Fort Erie, Ontario
Buffalo, NY 14240	L2A 9Z9

BN-Jan-2

Please send me my Special copy of the Betty Neels Treasury Edition. I have enclosed the four Treasury Edition coupons required and $2.95 for postage and handling along with this order form. (Please Print)

NAME_____

ADDRESS_____

CITY_____

STATE/PROV._____ ZIP/POSTAL CODE_____

SIGNATURE_____

This offer is limited to one order per household.

SUPPLIES LIMITED

This special Betty Neels offer expires
February 28, 1987.

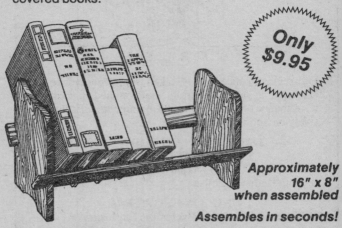